Praise for Elizabeth Maddrey

Book One: "Wisdom to Know"

"Elizabeth Maddrey has earned a spot on my 'must read' list, and I'm eager for the second book in her 'Grant Us Grace' series. She's able to be bold about the truth without becoming preachy or cliché, and real enough that any reader can relate to the story. My hope is that God uses her writing for both entertainment and ministry... you'll find powerful healing in these pages." – Deena Peterson

Book Two: "Courage to Change"

"I'm fast becoming a fan of Elizabeth Maddrey with her 'Grant Us Grace' series. I was surprised that the storyline centered on Allison but the transition from the first book was smooth and convincing. I feel like this series of books should be in each Crisis Pregnancy Center library. The book examines all the pros and cons of adoption. There were some sad and poignant parts as the characters portrayed life among real families. Families who sometimes want to control adult children and the painful interactions between parents and children. It also shows some of the prejudices that are prevalent even among church-going Christians. There are very good resources listed at the back of the book as well as discussion questions for Book Clubs. I'm looking forward to reading the next book in the series and would recommend this book to friends." – Donna Collins Tinsley

Book Three: "Serenity to Accept"

I love when I can relate to a story and its characters, especially ones where matters of faith are central--and "Serenity to Accept" is one of those stories. What did I relate to? First of all, the characters. These were my family, friends, colleagues and even a few people in my life I wish I didn't know. Real world people, with real world issues using real world dialogue. Elizabeth Maddrey does a masterful job of engaging the reader with her people. I could also relate to the challenges these characters faced. One, as someone looking into issues of God AND as a devoted Christian living in a highly secular world. Nothing cookie-cutter. No pat answers. Real stuff. Just people--sinners all--muddling through an imperfect world, looking for--and finding--glimpses of an all-loving Savior. And that is why YOU should read this book!" – Connie Almony

For the most recent listing of all my books, please visit my website.

Joint Venture

A 'Grant Us Grace' novella

By Elizabeth Maddrey

For my sister – I couldn't do this without you.

Chapter 1

Outside Washington D.C., January, 2009

Ryan's cell phone vibrated. Laura Willis peered across the table at the screen. Should she answer it? She chewed her lower lip. On the one hand, he was her fiancé. On the other it was his phone, not hers. She'd answer it. As she started to reach for the phone, she glanced across the crowded restaurant. Ryan emerged from the hall that led back to the restrooms. An involuntary smile bloomed on her face, cell phone forgotten. How had she ended up with a man so handsome? Tall and slim, his brown hair was always perfect. She could see the perpetual hint of mischief in his green eyes as he stopped to slap the backs of some coworkers congregated at the bar. He said something that had everyone turning her way and laughing. Were they laughing at her? With a casual wave at his friends, he ambled back toward their table.

His piercing gaze hit her like a caress and she swallowed. How amazing was it going to be to be married to him? To not have to fight so hard to keep things from going too far? The wedding in June couldn't come fast enough.

"Miss me?" Ryan slid into the booth bench across from Laura and checked his phone. A tiny wrinkle formed between his eyes as he saw the missed call. Flicking his gaze to Laura, he palmed the phone and tucked it into his pants pocket.

"Oh, of course." Laughing, Laura sipped her water. "Can we talk invitations now, or did you want to wait until after the food came?"

"Invitations? C'mon, Laura. We've got six months, we don't need to decide so fast."

She gritted her teeth and forced a reasonable tone. "June'll be here before you know it. The catalogs all say to allow six to eight weeks for processing, so that's two months right there. They need to be mailed six weeks out, maybe seven. Plus I want to hand address them, which'll take at least a week with the number of people on the guest list…"

Ryan raised his hands in surrender. "Fine. Geez. Show me what you want."

Fighting to hide disappointment about his attitude, Laura slid a dog-eared catalog out of her purse.

"My three favorites are these." She arranged the pages so all three could be seen at the same time.

He barely glanced down, his gaze fixated above her and slightly to the left, where a TV suspended from the ceiling was showing a basketball game. "That's fine."

"Which one?"

He shot her a disgusted look and studied the catalog for all of ten seconds before poking the middle one. "That one. Happy?"

Great. Her least favorite. She opened her mouth to discuss the other two, but his attention was already glued back on the game. Fine. They'd have funeral flowers on their invitations. She'd only included the calla lilies option because her mother liked it. Ryan knew how she felt about lilies and weddings…had he chosen it to make a point? She folded the catalog open. Maybe she'd just choose her own favorite after all. He wasn't likely to remember what he'd pointed at anyway.

"Thanks." She cleared her throat. "Do you want traditional wording or something a little more personal?"

Ryan sighed and shook his head. "Really? There's more?"

Laura scooted the three wordings she'd typed up across the table, taking care to put the one she liked best in the middle. He jabbed the middle one with his index finger. She was right, he wasn't even looking.

"Satisfied? Are we done with wedding business now? I'd like to enjoy our date, not get nagged about nitty details."

"Sure." Laura busied herself tucking the wedding information back into her purse. Tears welled in her eyes. It was silly to be upset. Hadn't everyone told her men didn't care? And here she was, pushing. "Excuse me a minute, would you?"

Laura grabbed her bag and escaped to the bathroom where she held a wet paper towel over her eyes. What was with Ryan? Every time she tried to talk about the wedding, he got angry or distant. He'd proposed a year ago and then, despite her best efforts, pushed for a long engagement. He'd said it was to save up money so they could buy a house as soon as they were married, but as far as she'd seen, she was the only one saving. He'd just gotten back from another guys-only vacation to Las Vegas and, from what she'd pieced together, had footed most of the bills.

She checked her makeup and tossed the paper towel in the trash. No more wedding talk tonight. Maybe then he'd tear his eyes away from the excitement of a dribbling ball and they could at least spend some time talking. Resolute, Laura headed back to the table. When she got to the main room, she stopped. Who was that at their table?

She skirted around the bar, hoping to keep out of Ryan's line of sight. The woman in Laura's seat leaned across the table and stroked Ryan's cheek.

Laura's mouth dropped open as he glanced around before leaning in and kissing the other woman. The juicy kiss went on. Her stomach stirred, bile burning the back of her throat. Straightening her spine, Laura wrenched the diamond solitaire off her finger and marched toward the table.

"How dare you?" Laura hissed and grabbed a handful of blonde hair, yanking apart the woman and Ryan. And then she recognized the woman. Betrayal intensified her nausea as the blood drained from her face. "Lydia? How could you?"

"It's not what it looks like..." Ryan trailed off when Laura glared in his direction.

Laura cocked back her arm and let her fist fly, powered by her legs and back. It connected with a satisfying crunch. Ryan's hands flew to his face, sputtering as blood flowed from his nose. She flung the ring at him and stormed from the now silent restaurant.

Laura unlocked the salon door and reached for the bank of light switches. Kicking the door closed behind her, she flipped the deadbolt and surveyed the room. Janelle, the assistant manager responsible for closing last night, had done her usual sloppy job cleaning. In general, Laura would have let everyone do their part when they got in, but she'd given up trying to sleep at three a.m. and as soon as the clock hit six had gone ahead and gotten up. Now, at seven, she had a solid two hours before even the earliest stylists would be in, and the first appointment on the books wasn't until ten.

She dropped her purse at her station and planned. She'd start with the mirrors and surfaces, that way when she did the floors she'd get all that dust as well. At least there wasn't still hair on the floor. Janelle had been known to sweep piles into the corner and then try to hide them behind a trash can. Why Brenda, the shop owner, kept Janelle on staff was a mystery to Laura.

As she sprayed and wiped the mirrors, the thin indentation on her naked ring finger screamed for attention. What was she going to tell her parents? They loved Ryan. Maybe even more than she did. Or had. The first time he cheated, Laura had been ready to wash her hands and move on, but her mother had insisted it wasn't worth throwing away so many years of a relationship for one indiscretion. There had been a few telling looks between her parents that Laura chose to ignore. Was infidelity just the way things were? She didn't want to believe it. Nor had she pushed. If her parents had that in their past and had worked through it, well, she was glad. But she wasn't going to be a doormat any longer.

She'd scoured the left side of the salon and was wiping down the reception desk when a flicker of movement caught her eye through the plate glass. She watched as Matt Stephenson, another stylist, pushed his key in the lock.

"Morning. You're here early." Matt kicked the door closed behind him and clicked the lock.

Laura smiled. He didn't look like your typical hair stylist. Tall and muscular, he was equally at home on the football field and behind a salon chair. It was an appealing combination.

"I could say the same. I figured I had at least thirty more minutes of quiet before anyone showed up."

Matt crossed to his station and set down his backpack. "Want me to put the coffee on?"

Laura gave the front desk a final swipe with her rag then moved to the first station on the right side of the room to begin a thorough cleaning. "It's already on. I needed a cup before I started on this."

"What time did you get in?"

She didn't look up from her scrubbing. "Seven. Given the state of things, it's good I did. I'm not sure what the cleaning crew has been doing, but cleaning isn't part of it."

Matt let out a short laugh. "You must have missed the memo."

"Memo?" Laura moved to the next station. "From Brenda?"

"Yeah. When you get a minute, you should check the board by the coffee in the employee room."

Laura cringed. What cost-cutting measure had Brenda decided on now? The salon wasn't doing poorly, but it wasn't a rousing success, either. Laura did fine, but that was primarily because she had a full schedule of very loyal clients, not because Brenda's House of Hair was anything special. "I'm assuming it has something to do with cleaning...let me have it."

"Ding. Got it in one. Brenda, in her infinite wisdom," Matt's voice seeped sarcasm, "has cut the cleaning crew back to once month and instructed stylists to care for their own station each night in the interim."

Laura's jaw dropped. "Once a month? How...what...why?"

Matt lifted a shoulder. "Can't answer any of those for you. Though I'm sure it's to do with the bottom line. Or, I should say, *her* bottom line. If she'd just start taking clients again, or more than one client a week, she could be doing much better."

"I'm going to check my rental agreement. I'm pretty sure regular cleaning was one of the perks she offered when I was shopping around for a place to build my client list." Laura shifted to the last station.

"It is, but unfortunately it's listed just like that, 'regular cleaning.' So technically, once a month, provided it's scheduled, qualifies. My space is up for renewal in April. I'm not sure I'm going to stay."

Laura's heart sank. Matt was her only real friend at the salon. She got along okay with the other stylists, but no one else was a Christian and there was too much gossip and backstabbing for her to consider any of them actual friends. What would the days be like without his humor to lighten the work? Especially now that her personal life was in tatters. "Keep me posted. And if you do leave...let me know if they might have space for me."

She headed into the back room and dropped the spray bottle and rag into the sink. Grabbing the broom, she went back out into the main area of the salon and attacked the floor at the front, dragging a growing pile of dirt, lint and hair toward the back. Should she look into leaving Brenda's? She didn't mind pitching in to help clean. But it seemed few others were doing their part, and weren't likely to if they knew she'd do it all. Brenda had leased her the space two years ago when Laura's license was sparkly new and she had very little in the way of recommendations. Now she had a full client load—overfull some days, which helped out the other stylists. She'd done right by Brenda. Could she say the reverse was true?

The majority of her clients would follow her. She wasn't worried, really, about losing business if she moved. Still, it felt like starting over. And maybe since the rest of her life was in an uproar she ought to keep one part of it steady.

Matt dropped the dustpan in front of her and held it still. "Here, let me help with that. Then you go ahead and get set up, I can do the mopping."

Laura glanced at her watch. The other stylists would be arriving any minute to start setting up their stations. "Tell you what, why don't you mop front to middle and I'll do back to middle and we'll get it done in half the time. Then we can be set before everyone else comes in, saving them from having to pretend they would've helped if they'd only known."

Matt chuckled. "Fair enough, I'll go fill some buckets."

Chapter 2

Matt glanced at Laura as she set up her station. Other than a smudge of black under her eyes, she appeared upbeat as always, but her engagement ring was conspicuously absent. She'd been wearing the thing, without fail, since the day she got it. Was there trouble in paradise? He smothered the urge to smile. It wasn't right to take pleasure in someone else's discomfort, but if Ryan was suffering, Matt was going to savor it.

He and Ryan had been friends in high school. Then Matt made the mistake of mentioning that he was going to ask Laura to Homecoming their Senior year. Before he could work up the nerve, Ryan swooped in. Ryan and Laura had been together since, even though it was no secret Ryan continued to play the field when he'd gone away for college and Laura had stayed home, working, going to beauty school, and being a faithful long-distance girlfriend. She deserved so much better. Maybe there was still a chance for her to have it.

Matt finished with his station set up and plopped into his client chair. "How's your week looking?"

Laura glanced up from arranging her scissors on a towel in front of the mirror. "I'm pretty booked, actually. I have seven today and at least five all the other days. What about you?"

"Not quite that many, but I'll stay busy enough. Let me know if you need help with shampoos or rinses."

"Thanks. Matt…" Laura trailed off as the front door opened and Brenda, followed by three of the other stylists, clattered in with loud greetings. "Never mind."

"Kevin?" Matt kicked closed the door to the townhouse that he rented with his best friend and dropped his gym bag before toeing off his shoes and pushing them out of the way.

"In the basement."

Matt bounced down the stairs and burst out laughing. His friend was sprawled on the couch, a laptop balanced on his chest. "Comfy?"

"I sit at a desk all day. I figure when I'm home I can do what I want." Kevin sat up, setting his computer aside. "What's up?"

Matt shrugged, flicking his gaze to Kevin's monitor. "You don't really want gossip from the beauty salon, do you? What are you looking at?"

Kevin cleared his throat. "I was thinking I might buy a house."

"Why?"

"Why not? I got a good bonus this year and it seems smarter to put it into real estate than the stock market. Plus, things with Lydia seem like they might finally be working out."

Matt sat on the coffee table. "Can you at least wait until our lease is up? We've got another six months before we lose our deposit... I'm not going to be able to handle the rent on my own and can't really afford to lose that money. Plus having time to find someplace else would be good."

"Yeah, of course. I'm just looking right now, it's not like I'm ready to put in an offer on anything."

Matt nodded, clamping down on the urge to say more about the house situation, even though it added another weight to his shoulders. "I'm staying in tonight. Want in on a pizza?"

"Definitely."

"I'll holler when it's here." Matt climbed the stairs, pausing on the main floor to get his gym bag before heading up to his room. Living on his own wasn't something he was looking forward to. He'd managed to avoid it thus far and had really hoped the next roommate he'd have would be his wife. With Kevin bailing and not even the prospect of a girlfriend...it was either find a new roommate or give solitary life a try.

He tugged the dirty clothes out of his bag and balled them up, shooting them into his laundry basket. He cupped his hands around his mouth, imitating the noise of a cheering crowd. Matt opened the web page for his favorite pizza place and logged in. He prized the convenience of Internet ordering. He could save his favorite order and have it coming his way with the click of three buttons. Kevin wasn't a huge fan of Matt's favorite Hawaiian pizza, but he knew better than to complain within earshot. Tapping a finger on the keyboard, Matt reviewed the order. After a moment's hesitation he added an order of cheese bread. That would ensure there was no griping.

He leaned his head back and stared at the ceiling fan. Before he'd gone to the gym, he'd stopped by two different salons that were advertising rental space. The first was so filthy he hadn't made it past the reception area. There was no way he was going to ask his clients to follow him into that. The second had potential, and there was space that Laura could rent as well, if she was serious about leaving Brenda's. Still, something had seemed off and he couldn't quite nail down what. Was it simply that change was hard, or was there something else?

Chair squawking as he shifted position, he opened his email and clicked through to the storefront listing he'd found when idly browsing last week. The space was incredible, at least in the photos, and some of the equipment from the previous salon looked like it was in good shape. That would cut down on some of the initial costs...if he was insane enough to actually consider striking out on his own. Was he? With the complication of needing to find a new place to live, now probably wasn't the time to do something risky like open his own business. But with Laura as a business partner...would she even be interested?

Before he could talk himself out of it, Matt composed a short email to the listing agent on the property asking to schedule a showing. If the space looked as good in person as it did in the listing, then he'd worry about what came next. The first salon he'd visited today was a good reminder that photos didn't always represent the true state of things. He opened the only document he kept on his desktop and sent it to the laser printer. He'd take it to Laura and see what she thought. He might not be able to make a salon work on his own, but with her, and her client base, it was a lot more realistic. Leaving the printer spewing paper, he shoved away from his desk and padded downstairs to wait for the delivery man.

Chapter 3

Laura pulled into the driveway and groaned. What was Ryan's car doing here? She'd wanted to get home and explain the situation to her parents. They'd still been out when she got home last night and she'd left early enough to avoid running into them, though that wasn't all that unusual. Living at her parent's home helped her save the majority of her meager paycheck, and it kept her mom from worrying about her. The down side, which so far they'd managed pretty well, was achieving an acceptable quantity of independence and privacy. Laura had intended her nest egg to go toward a house for her and Ryan. Now she'd figure something else out.

With a growl, she locked her car and trudged to the front door. Since Ryan had no doubt delivered his own lies to explain the restaurant tonsillectomy he'd been giving her former best friend, she probably had her work cut out for her. Because this time it was over.

She hadn't wanted to stay with him the first time he cheated, and only had because of her parents' insistence. But she deserved better. Even if no one else seemed to think so.

"We're in here, honey."

Laura followed her mother's voice into the sunroom that spanned the back of the house. Ryan was seated at the casual table, laughing with her mom and dad. Her blood began to boil. Had he no shame? She shot him a fiery glare as she crossed the room to give her mother a peck on the cheek.

"What's going on?" Laura settled into a wicker chair next to her dad, the farthest from Ryan she could manage without going to the other side of the room.

"Ryan just stopped by on his way home from work. He was saying he might see if he could take you out for dinner. Were there wedding things you didn't cover last night?" Laura's mom beamed at Ryan before turning a questioning gaze on Laura.

Laura pursed her lips. So he hadn't said anything to them. He must have figured out that she hadn't said anything yet either. It was surprising that he hadn't jumped in with a pre-emptive strike. Maybe he was sorry? Even as she thought it, Laura quashed the sentiment. She didn't care if he was sorry. Not this time.

"I don't think so, Ryan. But I appreciate the offer."

"Oh, honey, don't be that way. Your beau is here. Go out and have fun. You don't always have to be the first person in the salon you know."

"Mom." Laura cleared her throat and folded her hands on the table, making sure her newly naked left hand was on top. "It's not about the responsibilities I have at the salon. It's the fact that Ryan and I broke up last night." She twitched her head to the side. "Frankly, I'm surprised he's here."

"Babe. Come on. I came over to explain."

Laura held up a hand. "Save it. I'm not stupid enough to fall for it twice."

Visibly distressed, Laura's mom began to twitter nervously. "Oh, Laura. You really should listen to him. You know how you over react sometimes. And the wedding…it's so close now. Just think of how embarrassing it'll be to call off your engagement."

So he had indeed spun a story. "Embarrassing? You know what's embarrassing, Mom? Walking out of the bathroom in a restaurant filled with a number of people you know only to find your fiancé in a lip lock with your best friend." Laura turned to her father, fury flaming up inside her. "What about you, Dad? Are you more worried about your social standing than the fact that, apparently, your daughter isn't good enough to deserve someone who'll be faithful to her?"

"That's not what your mother meant and you know it." His voice was gruff and Laura noticed his hands had balled into fists. "But as it turns out, this time

I have to agree with you. Perhaps, Ryan, you should be on your way."

"Now, now." Laura's mother laid a restraining hand on her husband's arm. "Let's not be hasty. At your age…"

Laura shoved her chair back and stood. "Hasty? This is the second time…that I know about. I'm done. *We're* done." She stalked from the room, ignoring her mother's increasingly desperate pleas for her to come back and discuss things rationally. Rationally. Ha! She had been rational. If she'd done what she wanted to, Ryan would have another black eye. The fact that he'd been wearing concealer lifted her spirits. Jerk.

In her room, Laura grabbed her trash can and began dumping all of the wedding magazines and catalogs into it. She'd put them in the recycling bin later. At least she wouldn't have to deal with death lilies on her invitations after all. When the cleaning frenzy ended, a calm settled over her. She lay on her bed, staring up at the blank ceiling. Over the years, she'd had a number of posters up there. Usually one heart-throb actor or another. Until a few minutes ago, it'd been an engagement photo. Now she was going to consider it a representation of the future. Blank, but full of potential.

There was a light tap at her door and she bit back a groan. Why couldn't they just accept that she knew the right thing to do and leave her alone?

"Yeah?"

Laura's mom poked her head in. "Can I come in?"

She scooted to a sitting position and nodded. "'Course. Though I'll warn you now, I'm not changing my mind. So if that's what you're after, you might as well save your breath."

"No. No, your father's made it clear I'm not even supposed to try." She grimaced and perched at the foot of the bed, resting a hand on Laura's ankle. "But I do think you need to be sure you're sure. Ryan's got a good job. He could provide well for you. And it's not as if there are all that many other prospects out there."

Laura blinked, taken aback. "You don't know that. I don't even know that. I've been dating Ryan since my Senior year in high school."

"Yes, but at your age ..."

"My age? I'm twenty-three. I'm pretty sure that stopped being considered a spinster sometime early last century."

"It's just not as easy to meet someone once you're out of school. And you didn't even go to a proper college where you could meet eligible men."

Laura was unable to hold back her growl. Not again. Why was it that her mother thought she could do so much better in her career but not in her personal life? Where did the bizarre double standard come from? "Can we not? Please? It's going to be okay. Better than okay. I'm better off without him, Mom. We all are.

Though I am sorry to have upset your social calendar. At least we hadn't mailed the invitations yet."

Laura couldn't interpret the long look her mother gave her before squeezing her ankle and leaving the room. When the door snicked shut, she flipped onto her side and stared at the wall. She wouldn't worry about the future tonight. Everything was going to be just fine. It had to be.

Laura looked up from her novel as Matt pushed through the salon door and relocked it behind him. "You're early again."

"I could say the same…everything okay?" He crossed to his station and dropped his bag, kicking it under the mirror before sitting in his client chair and spinning to face her.

"Not really. We're friends, right Matt?"

He lifted an eyebrow. "I've always thought so."

She nodded. At least she had one friend. Lydia's betrayal left her unable to breathe. Most of the people in her social sphere were links from her relationship with Ryan or her friendship with Lydia. "Good."

"You wanna talk about it?"

Would it help any? She had brought it up, obliquely, by not just saying things were fine. She sighed. "I broke off my engagement to Ryan on Friday. Broke up with him, to be honest. He's cheating. Again. This time I caught him at it."

Matt's face twisted with sympathy. "Ouch."

"Yeah. Something like that. But it's good. It is. Better to know now when I can do something about it. Right?" She pulled her lower lip between her teeth. She believed it, but it still hurt.

"I guess. Better if he hadn't been cheating, I imagine."

The chuckle that escaped surprised her. "There's that. Anyway. I lost my fiancé and best friend all in one fell swoop. So...I'm mostly trying not to think about it. I know denial won't help forever, but right now it's working pretty nicely."

"Best friend. Lydia? He was cheating on you with Lydia?"

Laura's eyes closed and she gave a brief nod. "Can we change the subject? How are you? Any luck with a new salon space?"

Matt's gaze heated her skin. He looked like he wanted to say more and she really hoped he'd just let it go. She was caught in that strange space between violent anger and a need to weep hysterically. Any more talk about it was likely to push her one way or the other, and neither was productive right now.

After a moment he gave a slight smile. "Only if ruling places out counts. I visited one salon yesterday...it made Janelle look like a clean freak."

Laura winced. "Not possible."

"Oh, I would have agreed with you until I saw that place. I made it about four steps in from the door before I turned around. It's no wonder they have space available." He shook his head. "I visited another, and it's a possibility but...I don't know."

"I understand that. The fact that the places you visited were open on Sunday says plenty. Do you really want to work somewhere that's going to be expected? I looked at a bunch of places before settling on Brenda's. Some of them just didn't feel right." She sighed. Not that Brenda's was feeling all that right anymore. Not with Matt thinking about leaving.

He cleared his throat. "Yeah, open on Sunday's not a big draw for me. So...I'm going to look at another space tonight. It's..."

The bells on the door jangled as Janelle and the shampoo girl came in. Laura tucked her book into her drawer and rolled her eyes at Matt. "Tell me about it later. Or maybe call me when you're done?"

Laura flipped closed her phone and tossed it on her bed. Between Lydia and Ryan, the thing had been ringing since she got off work. There wasn't really anything she needed to say to either one of them, so she'd ignored the calls. They just didn't seem capable of taking a hint. She thought about just turning it off, but she didn't want to miss Matt's call. Assuming he actually did call. She couldn't decide why it mattered so much, but the thought of leaving Brenda's had become a lifeline, and she was clinging to it with everything she had. Even if she shouldn't throw more chaos into her life right now, she couldn't shake the idea that a completely new start was exactly what she needed.

The phone lit up again. Different number this time, at least.

"Hello?"

"It's not too late, is it?" Matt sounded excited. Maybe he'd found space. Laura hoped there was room for her, too.

"It's not even nine yet. I don't know anyone who goes to bed that early."

Matt chuckled. "Sorry. I lost track of time and didn't check before I dialed."

"Did you find something? You sound like you're ready to burst."

"Kind of…if it's not too late to call, is it too late to get some coffee, or ice cream or something?"

Laura was taken aback. Was he asking her out? Surely not. Even if he was, she just got out of a relationship, and it'd be stupid to jump right into a new one. Right? What was she even thinking? She and Matt were friends. He just didn't want to go over everything on the phone. Men hated talking on the phone, she knew that.

"Laura? You still there?"

"Yeah, sorry. Um." She glanced down at the yoga pants and t-shirt she was wearing. Not a date, just a friendly coffee. "Sure. Where should I meet you?"

Chapter 4

Matt tapped his fingers on the side of his coffee cup as he waited for Laura to arrive. He hadn't meant to ask her to coffee, but the words slipped out before he realized what he was saying. She'd taken so long to answer him…she probably thought he was hitting on her. Not that he'd mind asking her out for a real date, but she'd just gotten out of an engagement. Even he wasn't so clueless that he thought that dating immediately was a good idea. He'd just been so excited about the storefront…it had such great potential for a salon and spa. His mind was racing with the possibilities.

"Hey. Sorry, it took me a little longer than I thought. My mom got on my case about going out on a week night." Laura groaned. "I've got to get out of there. Let me grab some hot chocolate, then I want to hear all about it."

Matt smiled and watched as she ordered and paid. Should he have offered to get it for her? No. This wasn't a date.

"Okay." Laura slid into her seat and blew across the top of her cup. "What salon did you look at and do they have room for me?"

He cleared his throat and reached into the duffel bag he'd shoved under his chair to retrieve a manila folder. "Marcie's? Not too far from church."

Laura frowned. "Didn't they close last year?"

He nodded and slid the folder across the table. "I've always known I wanted my own place. Salon and spa. You remember I took the extra management classes?" When she nodded, he continued. "I've been working on a business plan for about six months and I think, with the right partner, it could work."

"Partner?" She glanced down at the folder then back at him. "Wait, me?"

"Is it crazy?" Matt held his breath as she opened her mouth and clamped it shut. Maybe this was a bad idea after all. "Too crazy. Look, don't worry about it."

She snatched the folder to her chest as he started to reach for it. "I didn't say that. I just hadn't thought about it. I mean, I thought about it as a down-the-line kind of thing. But right now?" She pursed her lips. "Why don't you run me through the highlights and I'll take this home to read more carefully."

He grinned. At least it wasn't an immediate no.

"How'd it go?" Kevin looked up from the sofa in the living room as Matt pushed the door shut behind him.

"Which part?" He toed off his shoes and pushed them against the wall before crossing the room and dropping into a chair. "The storefront is incredible. I still don't understand why Marcie's business went under. Well, that's not entirely true, but it wasn't the space that was the problem. There's a good sized main salon area with three rooms on one side that could be for treatments like facials and massages, and a decent area in the back that could be supplies, break room, and an office."

Kevin grinned. "Sounds perfect. Are you jumping on it?"

Matt frowned, wagging his head from side to side. "That's the part that I'm not sure went quite so well. You've seen my business plan…it's a lot to take on with just one person. I think I *could* do it, I'm just not sure how smart it would be. But with a business partner, someone who's got a steady, loyal clientele…then it starts to make a lot more sense. So I called to see if Laura might be interested in being a business partner."

"Laura from church and the salon? That Laura?"

Matt nodded.

Kevin's eyebrows shot up. "Would Ryan go for that, do you think?"

Matt cleared his throat. "Actually, I'm not sure how much that matters."

"They're engaged. It matters. You know Ryan."

"That's the thing. They're not engaged anymore. I thought you might have heard about it."

"Why would I have? Ryan and I have never been pals. As much as I like Laura, I don't understand what she sees in him. Or saw in him, I guess? Either way...I just don't get the hype. Besides, you know as well as I do that he was cheating on Laura in high school. And college. And every chance he got."

"Yeah. But this time she caught him in a lip lock."

Kevin snickered. "Serves him right. I feel bad for her, but I'm glad she saw the light."

Matt eyed his friend. Should he mention who the lip lock was with? If the situation was reversed, he'd want to know. Probably. "With Lydia."

Kevin sent him a questioning look.

"The lip lock. Ryan was kissing Lydia. Or vice versa. It was mutual, from what Laura said. Sorry, man."

Kevin frowned. "I...you're sure?"

"I only know what Laura said, and she didn't elaborate much. But she was pretty clear that it was

Lydia. She was doubly betrayed." Had he done the right thing in mentioning it?

Kevin scrubbed a hand over his face and threw aside the folder of papers he'd been reading. "Well. That kind of changes things."

"What things?"

"I mean there's really no point in rushing the house process—not that I was in a big rush, but I did feel a little urgency—if I totally misread the situation with Lydia. Which it seems I did."

"I'm sorry. Did you have someplace that you were leaning toward?"

Kevin shook his head. "Not really. And that was starting to get frustrating. So…maybe this is a good thing, somehow?"

Matt forced a smile. He didn't know what to say. He'd never been a big fan of Lydia, nor had he ever particularly thought she was the right person for Kevin. But Kev had been so sure since high school. Matt tried to be supportive.

"I think I'm going to head to bed." Kevin pushed himself out of the couch. "Let me know what Laura says about the joint venture. I think it sounds like a good deal, if my opinion matters."

Matt watched Kevin plod up the stairs. There ought to be something to say, or do. But what? He checked his phone. Nothing from Laura yet. Not surprising. There was a lot to read in the business plan. Then a lot to think and pray about. He winced. Prayer hadn't exactly been high on his own list of responses lately. But that could change right now. He stood and swung through the kitchen for a snack before heading to his room to take a meeting with God.

Chapter 5

Laura flipped the page. Admittedly, she hadn't read many business plans, but Matt's seemed to be thorough. He'd visited several local salons with day spas and somehow managed to pry financial information out of the owners. It was his charm. He could get you to agree to anything if you weren't careful. She'd been in a few situations with him where she'd been powerless to do anything other than go along with his plan. They'd all turned out fine, but it was good he didn't try to use his charisma for evil.

She chuckled at herself and turned the page, revealing a hand-drawn sketch on the back of, she flipped it over, a realtor listing. She went back to his notes and considered the floor plan he'd drawn in neat, steady lines. The concept was good, and it certainly looked like there would be enough room for a high quality salon along with treatment rooms. But did the neighborhood need another day spa? They seemed to be cropping up all over the place.

Laura was reasonably confident her clients would follow her. Except that Matt's plan called for the stylists to be employees, not individual owners renting shop space. Even before she'd read his carefully detailed explanation for the decision, she'd understood the rationale behind it. There were definite pros and cons. Pricing wouldn't be individual like it was now, which would mean some of the older ladies she saw each week might not be able to afford her services. She did their hair at a significant discount because it was a way to serve the less fortunate. And she enjoyed the time chatting with them. Would Matt let her continue to do that? Could they maybe have a senior discount that would apply to anyone?

She hopped off the twin bed that had been hers since she was in grade school and crossed to her desk. There had to be a pen here somewhere. She dug through the drawers filled with old papers and greeting cards she'd never send. Finally her fingers closed around a pen with bubble gum pink ink. It'd have to do. She curled back up on her bed and scribbled a note in the margin next to the proposed pricing. From a business owner standpoint, she wasn't sure about the feasibility of health insurance. She liked the idea that their salon employees could actually use the job to make a living, not just to supplement a husband's income. And that those without a husband wouldn't have to just pray they didn't get sick. But the cost. She skimmed the numbers and made another note in the margin. She'd want to take another look at that, maybe get a few other estimates.

She was half-way through the list of furniture that was available to purchase with the space, and Matt's thoughts on what they'd still need, before she realized she was already thinking about the salon as theirs. Was she really going to do this? She rubbed a hand across her stomach to ease the sudden tightness. If she was in, really in, she needed to be sure they were going to succeed. She couldn't handle another colossal failure in her life.

Laura pressed her fingers to her eyes. She wasn't a failure. Just because her mother still didn't understand why she'd let something as "insignificant" as Ryan kissing her best friend end her engagement didn't mean she was wrong to do so. Her dad had even taken Laura's side at dinner, and that hadn't happened in a very long time.

For whatever reason, Mother seemed to have forgotten that this wasn't the first time Ryan had cheated. Laura had forgiven him before and tried to act like nothing had changed, but it had taken her a while to stop wondering what he was doing when they weren't together. This time they'd been engaged. If he wasn't committed enough to be faithful when they were going to be married, what would keep him from cheating after they'd said their vows? And how would she ever learn to trust him again?

Laura pushed the thoughts aside. She had no intention of learning to trust him again. What was the saying? Fool me once...well, she'd accept the shame this time, but she was learning from it and moving on. The same applied, to some degree, to Brenda's. Even with the hours she'd spent cleaning the other day, things were already degrading on everyone else's station. She and Matt took time to clean up their areas each day and help with the floors, but no one else seemed to be interested in making a dent in the communal areas or even their own stations. If things didn't change soon the salon was going to be gross. She didn't want to work somewhere like that...and she didn't think her clients would put up with it either.

Which brought her back to the business plan. Was she ready to branch out on her own? It was less scary knowing it was a joint venture, but still. At least Matt was someone she trusted. She'd known him since high school, and while they hadn't really formed a friendship until trade school, he was the closest thing she had to a friend now that Lydia and Ryan were out of her life. There were worse things than going into business with your friend. She flipped back to the front page of the business plan. She'd pray about it. And read it through again, taking the time to work through the numbers on her own before she made a firm decision.

"I'm in." Laura dropped her marked up copy of the business plan on Matt's station as he packed up his tools at the end of a grueling day. Her feet were killing her. She'd been standing behind her chair non-stop all day. One of the other stylists called in sick but didn't bother to reschedule her appointments, so Laura had squeezed them in as she could. Matt had helped out when he had time, but no one else even offered. Then they'd all gone home as soon as their shift was over, leaving clients in the waiting area. Were they just lazy? Laura appreciated the extra money, but she also couldn't stand to think that a client would be turned away from the salon. Not after they'd taken the time to make an appointment. It wasn't their fault the stylist they'd chosen was irresponsible. And she wasn't going to close up until everyone had been seen. At least it gave her a chance to talk to Matt without anyone overhearing.

"Really? That's great." He nodded to the thick folder. "You can keep that."

"I made notes last night. I have some questions and some places where I think we need to re-strategize. And I want to see the space and equipment for myself. But first you should look that over and make sure you're okay with the changes. If you are, I downloaded some partnership paperwork from the Internet, made some tweaks and signed it. If you're not happy with it, we can hunt up an actual attorney, but that's going to cost more."

Matt grinned. "I'll look it over. In the mean time, I'll call the realtor and see about getting an appointment. Even moving quickly, I don't know that we'd be able to open before August. And that's being optimistic. But I'd want to lock in the space as soon as we can...can you swing that?" Laura nodded and Matt turned to call the realtor.

Laura'd prayed about start up costs last night and come to terms with using her nest egg. It hurt, more than she wanted to admit, to know her money wouldn't go to the house she and her husband would raise their children in. But since, at this point, there wasn't going to be a husband, or children, the money might as well do something besides collect dust and a measly one percent interest rate in her savings account.

Matt cupped his cell phone in both hands and turned back to her. "Are you in a hurry to get home? Macy, she's the listing agent on the salon space, might be able to get us in tonight. It's not like anyone's working there."

"Nothing pressing waiting for me. Get the appointment set up. I'm going to sweep up and do a little cleaning before things get so gross that I have to tell my clients to find a new stylist."

"I'll help as soon as I'm off the phone."

A hint of nausea rolled around in her stomach. Was she really going to do this? Laura rehashed all the reasons she'd listed the night before. Some of her nerves faded. It was a big step, but she was ready for some change in her life. Now that everything was falling apart, it was time to remake herself.

Matt crouched down with a dustpan as she swept the last corner and brought the hair and dirt to the pile she'd made. "She can meet us there around eight. Feel like grabbing dinner? We could go over some of your notes."

Laura glanced at her watch. It wasn't quite six. If she went home, she'd barely have time to sit before she had to turn around and leave. Plus her mother would grill her about where she was going. She wasn't ready to discuss the idea with her parents. Well, maybe her dad. But her mother would definitely not approve. She couldn't handle yet another argument right now.

"That works. Let me gather up the trash and make sure everything's off in the back room."

"What sounds good?"

Laura shrugged. "Whatever you're in the mood for is fine."

Laura slid down in the tub until only her neck and head were above the steaming water and frothy bubbles. A folder and a pile of catalogs perched on the edge of the tub — homework from the evening of salon-hunting with Matt. She smiled as she let her thoughts drift back over their time together. They'd ended up eating at a sandwich shop in the same shopping center as the potential salon space. Since they were going to be discussing the salon, Matt insisted on paying, reminding Laura he could write it off as a business expense. She hadn't wanted to agree, but it made sense. Still, there was the slim possibility that he had some notion of it being a date…and that was ridiculous. Just because he paid for dinner, with a perfectly legitimate reason, didn't mean he had romantic intentions. And she didn't need to make a fool out of herself by saying something just to confirm that. There was no point in coming across as either paranoid or vain. Or both.

The realtor had been late, but they'd spent some time browsing the other stores. It didn't feel like your typical strip mall. Each shop had a green and white striped awning with the store name printed on the flap and a large window. The awnings and the brick fronts combined to give the impression of a series of boutiques rather than a generic suburban shopping center. Most of the stores used the plentiful window space for displaying their wares in a creative manner, though a few simply let you peer into the shop with no obstruction. All of them, though, seemed to take pride in their business and aim for a more upscale clientele. That was definitely a bonus when you were considering putting in a salon and day spa. Why had the other gone out of business? She was going to have to see if she could track down the scoop. If there was something wrong with the location for their type of business, she wanted to know before they started spending money.

The space itself was divine. If Laura had tried to design the perfect salon, she probably would have laid out something almost identical. Still, she did see a few things she'd want to change. Matt seemed to think they were doable. The main issue would be getting permission from the landlord. As for the equipment the prior salon had left, some of it was worth keeping, but not as much as Matt had hoped. The more detailed inspection Laura did after touring the space had revealed that none of the chairs still lowered properly. They'd go up fine, but the releases were all stuck. It might be a simple matter to fix, but it might not. And once you spent the money to buy the chairs and try to fix them, you probably would've been better off just getting new chairs to start out. At least then you knew what you were getting.

When they'd parted ways, Laura had promised to start pricing out the equipment they'd need now that they knew what they could and couldn't use from the previous salon. In addition, she was going to start figuring out what product lines they should carry. She knew some brands offered better incentives when you agreed not to carry or use their competitors, but she wasn't sure how beneficial that was in the long run. And she had every intention of getting into that. Just as soon as her feet stopped complaining about her extra long day.

Chapter 6

Matt kicked off his shoes as he shut the front door. Kevin's car was in its spot, but there weren't any lights on. It was only nine thirty. Kevin couldn't possibly be in bed already, could he? Matt swung through the kitchen and grabbed a soda from the fridge before trudging upstairs. His feet were killing him, as was his lower back, but a surge of excitement shot through him when he thought about the new salon. And he wanted to share that with his best friend.

Light spilled into the hallway from under Kevin's door, so Matt knocked.

"Yeah, come on in."

Matt pushed open the door to the master suite. Kevin sat in his office chair with his feet up on his desk, laptop balanced on his thighs.

"You're home late."

"I took Laura to see the potential salon space. She's interested." Matt slumped to the floor and leaned against the bookshelves that lined the short wall of the room.

Kevin grinned. "That's great. What'd she think of the location?"

"Seemed to like it, though she did a much more thorough inspection of the equipment they left and most of it isn't going to be worth buying. That's going to inflate the start up costs some. She said she had catalogs at home and would put some numbers together tonight. So I guess we'll see where that lands us."

"Better to know now though." Kevin pulled his feet down and used the forward momentum to propel him close enough to the desk that he could set down the laptop.

"True." Matt pulled the joint venture paperwork out of the folder he'd brought in with him and slid it across the floor toward Kevin. "You know anything about legal partnerships?"

Kevin scooted to the papers and picked them up. "Hmm. Probably not as much as you need someone to know. This looks pretty boilerplate. But you should consult an actual attorney. I'm not sure, but given what you want to do, you might be better off incorporating."

Matt pressed his fingers into his eyes. "I was afraid of that. Know anyone you'd recommend?"

"Why don't you see if Allison knows someone? Surely she's got some contacts from law school, right?"

"That's not a bad idea. I'll shoot her an email. I think I still have her address."

"If you can't find it, let me know. I probably have it around here somewhere too."

Matt pushed himself to his feet and collected the papers. "Guess I'll go do that now and then get started on answering some of the questions Laura had on the business plan. I'll tell you one thing, she's not taking this lightly."

"Probably nice to have something to sink her teeth into after the breakup."

Matt winced. "Heard anything from Lydia?"

Kevin shook his head.

"Sorry, man."

Kevin shrugged. "What are you gonna do, right?"

Matt offered a sympathetic smile as he tugged Kevin's door closed and went into his own room.

Matt watched as the salon began to fill with sleepy stylists. Where was Laura? He'd been looking forward to the hour they shared before anyone got there. Not just to discuss the salon, though that was part of it. But he missed her smile and the hint of morning fog in her eyes that slowly cleared as she cleaned and set up her station. She wasn't classically beautiful, but she was everything he was looking for in a woman. And that wasn't a particularly productive train of thought. Especially when he spotted his first client of the day pulling into a parking spot and another person tugging open the door.

"Where's Laura?" Ryan settled, possessively, Matt thought, into Laura's client chair, and shot Matt a fulminating glare.

Matt shrugged and focused on not thinking of all the nasty words he wanted to call the man. Instead, after a deep breath through his nose, he asked, "Why are you here, Ryan?"

"Need a haircut. There's no way she'll turn away a paying customer. Anyway, I made an appointment. And she's late."

A blur in the parking lot caught Matt's eye. It was Laura rushing from the back of the lot, where Brenda insisted they park. He'd never particularly wanted to have telepathy until that moment. There had to be some way to warn her.

Laura grabbed the door and held it open for Matt's client. With only the briefest glare at Ryan, Matt headed to the front of the salon, raising a hand in greeting.

"Mrs. Morgan, it's so good to see you. I'll be right with you." Matt jerked his head at Laura.

She followed him behind the desk. Matt was grateful it was screened, somewhat, from the back of the salon.

"I'm not late." Laura hissed under her breath. "My first client isn't for another hour."

"Apparently you had something hit the books this morning, and it's not someone that you'll be happy to see."

Laura just looked at him, clearly confused.

"It's Ryan."

"He didn't."

"He did."

The color drained from her face. "What am I supposed to do? I'm not cutting his hair. I'm not even speaking to him. What is he hoping to prove?"

"I can't answer any of those for you. Sorry, Laura." Matt offered a tight smile. "At least you have a few minutes to think it over. I need to get Mrs. Morgan started though, it's her monthly color and curl today, not just a touch up."

Laura nodded, her face blank.

Matt squeezed her shoulder, wishing he could pull her in for a hug. Even if he thought Brenda, who'd been watching the whole exchange with narrowed eyes, would stand for it, he wasn't sure how Laura would react. And he didn't want to do anything that would upset her more. He forced a cheery smile.

"Mrs. Morgan, come on back."

"What are you doing here, Ryan?" Laura slid her purse under the counter of her station and fisted her hands on her hips.

"You aren't taking my calls. I need to talk to you, to explain, so you'll quit overreacting."

"Overreacting?" Heads started turning, so she forced her volume lower. "No possible reaction to finding you kissing my ex-best-friend not five minutes after we picked out wedding invitations can be considered overreacting."

Ryan made a dismissive wave. "She just stopped by to say hello."

"With her tongue?"

At least he had the grace to flinch slightly. It didn't make her feel any better, but honestly, did he really think she'd buy that lame excuse?

"I just need a trim."

"You know what? Fine. This way." Laura gestured toward the sinks. He followed to an empty station where she pushed him into the chair and circled around to the back. Grabbing a thick handful of hair, she pulled his head backward and flipped the water to hot.

"Tell me if this temperature doesn't work for you." It was so hot it hurt her hands, but he did nothing other than wince. She pumped two squirts of their most floral-smelling shampoo into her hands and began to scrub viciously.

"You need to be reasonable. Ow."

Laura kept her tone sweet as her nails dug into his scalp. "Is that so?"

"Yes. Ow. Honestly, Laura. It didn't mean anything."

"Ah. Changing tactics." Laura shook her head and flipped on the nozzle, smiling as steam billowed from the bottom of the sink. "I thought she was just saying hello. Which is it?" She finished rinsing and dropped a towel on top of his head, scrubbing out the excess water before pushing him forward. "Let's go."

She caught his wary glance as she laid out her scissors and razors on a clean towel.

"Aren't you just going to use the clippers?"

Laura paused with small, pointy scissors in her fist and aimed the tips at his face. "Are you a stylist now, too?"

When he hastily shook his head, she smiled.

"Now, I've always thought you needed a slightly different look to really capture your personality. So since you're finally in my chair, and why is it that you wouldn't let me do your hair when we were dating and engaged, but now that we've broken up—and that's a permanent situation, by the way—you're ready for me to do this for you?" She waited a breath before barreling on. "Doesn't matter. I'm just grateful to get this one, final, shot to make you look the way you ought." She shook out a cape and snapped it around his neck.

He reached up and tugged at the collar. "Too tight, Laura."

"Don't overreact. You don't want hair all over your shirt, do you?"

Ryan reached behind him and unsnapped the cape as he stood. "This was a bad idea." He narrowed his eyes at her. "It's clear you're not in a rational state of mind. Maybe this really is for the best."

She barked out a short laugh. "Get out of here, Ryan. Don't contact me again."

As he bolted for the door, Laura called after him, "The shampoo's on the house."

The morning sped by. Laura focused on each client with as much of her attention as she could manage, though one part of her mind kept reviewing the…altercation—there really wasn't a better word for it—with Ryan. It wasn't her most professional moment, by any stretch of the imagination, even if Matt had given her a thumbs-up behind his client's back when Ryan stormed out. What had Ryan been thinking? That she wouldn't cause a scene at the salon? Maybe before Brenda's latest nonsense that would've been true. But now? What was she going to do? Laura wasn't Brenda's employee, she rented space at a price about twenty-five percent more than other places she could have chosen. That used to be worthwhile given the professional cleaners and paid receptionist that Brenda provided. But the cleaning crew had been herself and Matt lately. And though nothing had been announced, the receptionist had been AWOL for nearly a week. Laura suspected the woman had been let go. Which meant the phone often went unanswered and clients could sit in the waiting area for much too long before they were noticed.

She gave her last client of the morning a sunny smile and pulled her thoughts back to the present. "You look amazing, Mrs. Grolsh."

"You're a miracle worker, Laura." Mrs. Grolsh turned to admire the sides and back of her hairstyle. "I don't know how you manage it, but I'd be lost without you. And at seventy, I figure I have most everything figured out."

Laura laughed and leaned down to give the woman a tight hug around her bony shoulders. "Let's go to the front and I'll ring you up."

When Mrs. Grolsh had paid and tucked a generous tip into Laura's hand over her objections,

Laura rolled her head, stretching her neck. It was nearly two. Mrs. Grolsh always arrived just before noon for her color and set. It was a nice way to end the morning, chats with the woman were delightful, but it made for a late lunch if the rest of her morning was busy. She didn't have another client on the books until three-thirty and there was no one waiting up front, which meant she got a chance to grab something to eat. She took the insulated bag from under her station and headed to the small back room that housed supplies. The tiny table shoved in between boxes was Brenda's concession to an employee area. She insisted the insignificant surface was plenty big for any breaks people might want to take.

The room was, thankfully, empty. Laura set the bag down and wedged herself between stacks of hair dye and towels to settle on the rickety folding chair. With a deep breath, she laid her head on her arms and, even as her eyes filled, reminded herself that she was done crying over Ryan. He wasn't worth it. Knowing it, even believing it, didn't stop the tears. She'd invested so much of her time, her love, her *life* in him. For what? No point going down that road again. It was done. And thank goodness she'd found out what kind of man he really was before she walked down the aisle. She pushed herself up. She'd eat and think happy thoughts about her full afternoon schedule and the possibility of opening her own salon with Matthew.

The door swung open and Brenda bustled in, a frown etched into her face. "Laura."

Laura bit back a sigh at Brenda's officious and disapproving tone and unzipped her lunch bag. "Hi, Brenda."

"You were late today."

She hadn't been. Not really. She was well ahead of the first appointment she'd known about, but it wouldn't do any good to mention that to Brenda, who obviously had something on her mind, so she offered a polite smile and lifted her brow.

"It's not our habit to keep clients waiting. Particularly new clients."

She couldn't stop the derisive snort. Clients ended up waiting for every stylist other than her and Matt with disgusting regularity. "I'll keep that in mind."

"He left before you cut his hair. Clearly he wasn't happy with the service you were providing." Brenda scowled. "How are we supposed to get repeat business when stylists behave unprofessionally?"

Laura shook her head. This was ridiculous. It was true, she'd not behaved as professionally as she ought, but Ryan surely deserved to be an exception. "I think, if you look, you'll find I have the most repeat business in the salon."

"That doesn't matter. You behavior this morning was unacceptable."

"Noted." She reached into her lunch bag and pulled out her sandwich. When Brenda didn't move, she looked up. "Was there something else?"

"I won't have this attitude in my salon. You're poisoning the atmosphere for everyone and I just won't have it."

"So you said. I can assure you, so long as Ryan never shows his face in here, it won't happen again." Laura took a bite and forced herself to chew, despite the fact that it tasted like dust. There was no way she was responsible for the poisonous attitude in the salon. That responsibility lay solely at Brenda's feet and it had started well before her cost saving methods kicked in. The commission Brenda took on Laura's clients had to add up to at least a third of Brenda's income. The commission Brenda took from Matt couldn't be much less. They were the two most reliable stylists renting at Brenda's. With the benefits decreasing by the day, Brenda's attitude made Laura's blood boil.

Brenda stared. "You don't get it, do you? This salon is about more than you. This is a place for serious hair professionals to ply their trade. If you can't be part of the team, then you have no business renting a booth."

Laura took another bite and tried to figure out exactly what that meant. "I'll admit I'm a bit lost, Brenda. I don't think there's anyone else who is more of a team player than me, except perhaps Matthew. If you ask anyone out there, they'll tell you the same thing. When was the last time you picked up a broom around here? Or answered the phone? Or did any of the things that you listed as your responsibilities in the contracts we all signed when we began renting here?"

Brenda slammed her hand on the table. "That's it. You're done. Pack your tools and leave my salon. I'm terminating your rental agreement."

As soon as Matt had given her his business plan, Laura had read over her contract so the terms were fresh in her mind. She set down her food and arched a brow. "That's certainly your right. As I have six months left on my current lease agreement, per our contract, I'll expect not only a refund of my initial deposit but half of my rental fees for those six months."

Brenda spluttered. "You're not entitled to anything. In fact, I think you owe me for early termination."

Laura shook her head and kept her tone even, despite her flaring anger. "I'm not the one asking to terminate my lease. You're executing the eviction clause, without demonstrable cause. If you go get your copy of our contract, I'll point out the exact paragraph where it spells out what you owe me."

Brenda's voice rose, landing just shy of a scream. "I don't owe you anything. I gave you a spot when no one else would have you and you repay that by mistreating clients and badmouthing the salon? Get out. Pack your tools and get out. You'll get nothing from me. And if you steal any of my clients, I'll see you in court."

Laura dropped her half-eaten lunch into the bag and zipped it shut. "If that's your stance, then you will see me in court, for breach of contract. And don't think you won't be hearing from my attorney." She grabbed the bag and squeezed through the teetering stacks of supplies and back out into the salon.

The salon was silent. Stylists stared, open mouthed, as Laura walked to her station and began packing her tools. She'd call the clients she had scheduled for this afternoon and offer to come to them. She'd done hair in people's houses before and she could do it again.

When she'd collected everything that was hers, and not anything that could possibly be construed to belong to Brenda, she turned to Matt.

"Call me when you get off, would you?"

Chapter 7

Matt made himself focus on his clients not the clock. He'd heard the bulk of Brenda's conversation with Laura. Heck, most of the salon had overheard them. Well, they'd heard Brenda. Laura had kept her voice down most of the time. He'd gotten a little more information from the two clients who, for whatever reason, hadn't been able to reschedule with her and so Laura had sent them to him. After his last client, Matt had tried to hurry out, but Brenda had kept him, and everyone who was still there, doing little pointless things until an hour after they'd locked the doors. Usually stylists had some flexibility with their hours. They weren't employees after all. Brenda had hinted that might be changing. Matt wondered if she knew how many stylists she'd lose that very day if she tried.

He dug his cell phone out of his pocket and started dialing as he walked to his car.

"Hey, Laura. Sorry it's so late, still okay to call?"

"Yeah. How much could you all hear?"

Matt clicked the unlock button as he neared his car. "Most of what Brenda said. Less from you, though there were some bits here and there. Did she really say you weren't a team player?"

"Apparently. I just wonder who she thinks has been cleaning the salon the past week."

"If it's any consolation, a number of the other stylists who got held after to help with the cleaning hadn't realized how much work was going on."

"Not really, no. Didn't they ever have to clean up in school?"

Matt laughed and turned on the engine. "Who knows?"

"Anyway. What do you say to moving up our schedule some?"

"What do you mean?"

"Well, if I'm not working at the salon, I could be onsite at the shop managing any construction and handling deliveries. So we wouldn't have to do most of it on weekends. I can even do some of the work, like painting, and save us a little money."

"You're not going to find somewhere else?"

Laura's heavy sigh had Matt pulling the phone away from his ear and putting it on speaker. "I could, I guess. But then I'd just end up quitting in August. That doesn't seem like the smartest thing."

"What about your clients?"

"Well...that depends on a lot of different things. But I figured maybe I could carve out a little space in the new shop, cordon it off somehow, and take clients one or two days a week while we were getting started up."

"Hmm. We'd have to look at the legalities of that, but I don't have a problem with it if it'll work."

"Okay...so what do we do? We're doing this, right?"

"Yeah, yeah we are." Matt cleared his throat. "Tell you what, why don't you and I each put together a list of what needs to happen next and then tomorrow, no tomorrow won't work I've got a ball game after work."

Laura snickered.

"I know, I know, but I don't want to bail on the guys. What about Friday night? Busy?"

"No plans, no."

"How about we get together Friday night then? Dinner and we can go over our checklists and put together a plan of action. That gives me a little time as well to hit up the lawyer referral I got from Allison, you remember her, right?"

"Sure. That's right she's an attorney now. I might need to call her myself."

"She gave me someone who can help us figure out what kind of legal paperwork we need to get taken care of, hopefully."

"Sounds good. So…Friday?"

"Yeah, say seven?" Matt turned into the driveway of his town house and reminded himself that it wasn't a date. No matter how much he might wish it could be. He agreed to Laura's suggestion of takeout at his place so they could spread out and talk about whatever they needed.

He pushed end and turned off the car. They were really doing this. Something seemed to be stuck in his throat. There were a lot of details to take care of. Could they really get a salon off the ground in just a few months? He'd thought August would be pushing it. Of course, that was when they were both going to be working at Brenda's full time. The idea that things would be going so much faster was hard to wrap his mind around.

"You're home late." Kevin sat in the living room with Lydia.

Matt shook his head. "Brenda's losing her mind. Or she's given up on keeping any stylists whatsoever in her salon. Either way, she kept us all late, after having yelled at Laura while the salon was open all because Ryan showed up unannounced this morning and, as you'd imagine, Laura wasn't all that happy to see him." He flicked his gaze to Lydia and cringed. "And now that I've opened my big mouth, I'm going to just put the rest of my foot in there and say that I don't think you should be here."

Lydia's jaw dropped.

"Matt." There was no mistaking the warning in Kevin's tone.

"What? She's dating Laura's ex-fiancé. And she's the reason for the ex being out there in front. I can't think of any possible reason she's continuing to hang out here with you, leading you on."

"Matt." Kevin's voice was almost a yell.

"Leading him on? We're friends. I'm allowed to have friends, aren't I? Besides, I'm not dating Ryan."

"Just making out with him in restaurants, then?"

Lydia stood, gesturing for Kevin to stay quiet. "Look. Laura needed to know that Ryan would cheat on her with anyone that showed even the smallest interest."

"And your version of telling her about that was an in-person demonstration, set up for maximum humiliation? Nice."

Lydia shook her head. "Humiliation wasn't my intention. But she didn't hear me when I tried to talk to her about it."

"I find that hard to believe. You were her best friend. I can't imagine her ignoring you when you said, point blank, that Ryan was continuing to cheat on her."

"Well...maybe not if I'd been that straightforward. But I didn't want to hurt her."

Matt snorted. "I see. Well, if it's any consolation, she's not just hurt now, but pretty close to destroyed." He watched the color drain from Lydia's face and guilt for his harsh words tugged at his heart.

Then he remembered Laura's face when she saw Ryan and quashed it.

"That's enough, Matt." Kevin stood, placing his hand in the small of Lydia's back. "Come on, Lyd, I'll take you home."

Lydia nodded, moving toward the door as if in a daze. Kevin frowned at Matt, shaking his head and mouthing, "Not cool, man."

Matt watched them leave and sighed, running a hand through his hair. He could've handled that better. Of course he could have. But Laura deserved to have someone stand up for her, to realize how special, how worthwhile, she was. He didn't see anyone doing that, and it broke his heart. It wasn't as if he'd been carrying a torch for her since high school. He absolutely hadn't been. He didn't think he'd ever had a torch, especially not if he compared it to Kevin and Lydia. They were friends. That's all.

Friday dragged even more than Thursday had. Brenda was on a tear at the salon, reaming out the stylists who expected the cleaning to be done by someone else or who didn't pop up quickly enough when the bell at the door signaled a new client. The only positive Matt could find in the situation was that Brenda was actually in the salon. That was a distinct switch from recent months. Now he found himself wishing she'd go back to not caring about things.

Matt checked his watch as he climbed the stairs to his room. He wanted to shower and change before Laura came over to talk about the salon. Not that this was a date. He knew it wasn't. Didn't even want it to be. Or that's what he planned to keep telling himself. Maybe after some time he'd believe it.

The doorbell rang as Matt hung his towel up on the hook in the upstairs hall bathroom that was his. He hurried to comb his hair before skipping down the stairs, muttering to himself, "Business meeting. Not a date."

"Hi." He grinned as he opened the door.

Laura stood on the stoop loaded down with two reusable shopping bags from the local grocery store. She had on dark jeans and a bright pink sweater that highlighted her china-doll complexion. Something in his chest constricted.

She smiled, eyebrows raised. "Can I come in?"

"Of course, yeah. Sorry." Matt stepped back. "Can I take those for you?"

"Nah, I've got it. Can you point the way to the kitchen? I went ahead and made dinner, figured it'd be nicer than pizza or Chinese." She flashed a grin.

Why hadn't he thought of that? He could have offered to make something. Not that anything he would have thrown together would taste as good as what she'd brought smelled.

"Thanks." Matt was grateful Kevin was a bit of a neat freak about the kitchen table. "I'll get plates and stuff, let me know if you need help finding anything you need."

"We should be set – it's ready to go. Just...maybe serving spoons?"

Matt pointed to the skinny drawer by the stove. "All the utensils are in there. Hopefully you'll find what you need. If not, we can improvise."

Laura laughed. "I'm not sure why I expected anything else from two bachelors."

He set out two plates, glasses, and silverware. She looked comfortable in the kitchen. Did she like to cook or was it just something she did from necessity? Matt could find his way around, but given the option he'd always opt for ordering in or going out. Maybe it was time for that to change. His mother had given him basic cooking lessons...how hard could it be to expand on those?

When Laura had set out the plastic containers of steaming slices of roast beef swimming in thick gravy, green beans, and rolls whose tops were glistening with butter, Matt pulled out a chair and gestured for her to sit.

"This looks incredible. I may officially be too spoiled to have takeout again."

Laura laughed. "Somehow I doubt that, but I appreciate the sentiment."

Matt sat in the chair across from her and bowed his head, offering a short blessing over the food and their business planning. Inwardly, he added a stern half-prayer, half-reminder that this wasn't a date and he shouldn't read anything into it.

"So, how are things at Brenda's?" Laura slid the container of beans closer and dished some onto her plate.

Matt shook his head as he spooned extra gravy over his slices of beef. "Worse than I can remember it being. I'm not sure what happened, but it's like Wednesday flipped some kind of switch in her head and now she's gone completely off the deep end. Serena and Riley are already talking about leaving. They're just starting to realize who was doing all the cleaning and they're not excited about being responsible for their own station deep scrubs."

"Hmm. They're decent stylists, though neither has overly much ambition. What's their client base like, do you know?"

Matt chewed, thinking through the last week. "Not huge from what I can tell. I'd say they probably have a small group of loyal clients, but mostly they take walk-ins. And not many translate into people who request them. I'm not sure if that's because they're not happy with the cuts or because they manage to sneak back as walk-ins and still get one or the other."

Laura leaned over and pulled a legal pad out of the bag by her seat. She flipped several pages up before scribbling something on them. "We'll keep them in mind. I suspect they'd do better as full employees, where all they have to do is focus on hair and not worry about the business end of things. Especially since I was thinking," she looked up and flashed a rueful grin, "is it okay to start talking business?"

"Of course." Matt craned his neck to see what was on the paper.

Laura laughed and moved the pad so he could see it. "If you can read my handwriting, you're welcome to. I just put their names down. Anyway, I was thinking that our policy should be to assume a re-schedule with the same stylist as part of the check out process. That way people don't forget to rebook until their hair is dreadful and we can help stylists build their client base without much effort. If they're happy, obviously."

"And if they're not?" Matt sopped up the last of his gravy with a roll.

"Then I'm thinking we offer them a complimentary re-schedule with either you or me. That way, even if they end up not coming back, it's not going to be because we didn't do everything we could possibly think of."

Nodding, Matt eyed the container of beef. There were three slices left and, while he didn't want to be a pig, he hadn't had a roast this good since he last ate at his mom and dad's. Laura pushed it toward him.

"Just finish it off. I was going to leave the leftovers for you anyway."

"You're the best." He grinned and slid his plate out of the way to eat out of the container. "I like that policy idea though. I'll admit I haven't spent a ton of time thinking through the employee handbook aspect of things. I figured that would come down the line."

Laura chuckled. "Better to start out with it in place, I think. So I've put some notes together and can work on it while managing the construction and so forth." She stood and stacked his plate on top of hers then piled the empty containers on top of that stack and carried it all to the sink.

"Just leave them in there. I'll clean up later."

"You sure? It won't take long."

"I'm sure. You brought dinner; you definitely don't have to clean up, too. Plus, you're here so we can hammer out business details, not to do my dishes." Matt hoped his smile made it clear he was trying to be funny. The jittering in his stomach had amplified and he was starting to worry he was going to be ill. Not really what you wanted when someone brought you a delicious meal.

"All right." Laura pursed her lips. "Should we sit here or did you want to go into the living room?"

"Here's probably better." Matt knocked on the table. "More room to spread out and easier to write things down."

She grinned and returned to her seat before grabbing the stuffed bag by her chair.

"Before we get into all that," Matt nodded at the bag, "I spoke with Macy about the space and she talked to the owner. They're actually thinking of divesting that property, which means we could lease like we were planning or...they're taking purchase offers."

Laura's eyebrows shot up. "Wow. They'd split it up?"

He nodded. "Apparently two of the other shops have already purchased their spaces. Everyone is getting a chance to buy. If they pass, then the current owner will sell the remaining spaces, with current leases, to another property conglomerate."

"Can I just say 'wow' one more time? That...that's going to shift a lot of the figuring I did." She dug into her bag and pulled out a thick, stapled packet of papers and slid it across to Matt. "We'd need to think about upkeep and maintenance versus rental...but gosh the idea of owning our space is thrilling."

Matt chuckled and looked up from the printed spreadsheet. "Isn't it? I spoke to my bank, we were going to need a business loan anyway...adding in a mortgage, particularly if we can swing a decent down payment, isn't outside the realm of possibility. And, before you say anything, I talked to Kevin about possibly borrowing from him for the down payment. He was thinking of investing in a house—long story there that I'm not going to get into—but for now that's tabled. But he still wants to invest in something so, he's considering it."

Laura cleared her throat. "We probably don't even need him to invest." She dug into the bag again and emerged with her check book. She held it against her chest for a moment before flipping it open and angling it to where he could see.

Matt eyes widened. "What…?"

She laughed. "I live at home and I've been saving for a wedding and a down payment for our first house." She shrugged, but Matt could see the pain in her eyes. "Since I don't need it for that anymore, I'd just as soon invest it in a partnership that's going to work out."

He snapped his mouth shut on his initial instinct to say no. It was her money, and she could do whatever she wanted with it. And there was no question that it would make the mortgage reasonable. But…but what? Was it just that he didn't like to have so little to contribute? There was definitely an element of pride at play, no matter how much it galled him to admit.

"If you're sure that's what you want to do with it, I'm not going to tell you not to. But, I'll take the business loan out. That'll make the risk a little more equally split. And we're repaying you before we worry about the loan."

"That's ridiculous. The loan will have interest. I absolutely expect that we'll get the money out of the business—and I don't even think it's going to take that long—but we're not making bad business decisions just because I happen to have cash lying around."

"Okay. You're right." Matt ran his hand through his hair. "So are we buying? Is that what we're saying?"

She nodded, one corner of her mouth lifting into a grin. "I think so. I want to run a few more numbers, but yeah, I think we should make an offer and see where it takes us."

Matt stood and crossed to the refrigerator to pull out two sodas. He popped the top and handed one to Laura before opening his own. He held the soda up and waited for her to follow suit. "We're going to rock this."

Laughing, she tapped her soda can against his and drank.

Chapter 8

Laura slid into the pew next to Matt. "Can I sit here?"

"Of course." Matt shifted his Bible and small group study book to his other side. "Not sitting with your parents today?"

"I've decided that it's probably not going to be good press for the salon if I'm convicted of murdering my mother. So I'm working on making sure we have some time apart."

Matt cocked his head to the side. "Ryan still?"

"Ryan. Brenda. You." Laura waved her hands. "She's not happy about any of it. And all of it is, somehow, my fault. She thinks I need to forgive Ryan and marry him. That will, somehow, magically make Brenda renew my lease which will, in turn, get me away from my 'sweet' friend."

"By 'sweet' I'm guessing she's not saying I'm nice?"

Laura shook her head.

"You've told her I like girls, right?"

"I've tried. She just doesn't believe me."

"Well that's just…awesome."

Laura tried to hold back a snicker at Matt's expression that managed to combine both embarrassment and insult. Despite her best effort, a small noise escaped.

Matt glared. "It really isn't funny. Just because I do hair…"

"I know, I know." Laura offered a sympathetic smile. "I'll keep working on her. At least when it comes to you she keeps her thoughts to herself. She's told everyone about how I overreacted with Ryan. Honestly, you'd think he was her child, not me."

"Sorry." Matt reached over to squeeze her hand.

Laura started to speak, but the worship band drummer began clapping his sticks together to give the tempo for the first song. As they stood with the rest of the congregation, she tried to focus her thoughts on the words of the song, not the comforting warmth still radiating from her hand where Matt had squeezed it. It was a just a simple, friendly gesture. And even if it hadn't been, she was in no position to think about dating right now. She'd been with Ryan for so long and made so many plans for the future with him…it was time for her to make plans that were just for her for a while.

When the music finished, she sat and opened her Bible to the Gospel of Matthew, chapter six, along with everyone else and sighed when she saw the Lord's Prayer. Sure enough, Pastor Brown was talking about forgiveness. Wasn't there any time when it was okay not to forgive? Didn't she have a right to protect herself from a man who couldn't, or wouldn't, remain faithful? Annoyed, she flipped a few pages to the right and let her eyes skim the words. They were just random letters in odd combinations. Nothing made sense. She closed her eyes and let the pastor's drone slip over her. She didn't want to forgive Ryan. She wanted to find a sharp stick and poke him in the eye with it. Repeatedly. At least she'd gotten one good punch in. The memory of the bruising around his eye when he'd ambushed her at her house, and again at the salon, made her grin. She hoped it still hurt.

"Did I miss a joke?" Matt's breath tickled her ear and sent shivers down her spine.

She shook her head and opened her eyes. "No. Just...thinking."

Someone behind them pointedly cleared their throat. Laura hunched her shoulders and forced her attention back to the sermon, ignoring Matt's quiet chuckle and sing-song whisper of "Busted."

"Going to class?" Matt gathered his things and stood, arching his back until it cracked.

"I don't think so." Laura nodded toward the far side of the church where Lydia and Ryan stood talking with a group of singles from their class.

Matt winced. "You'll have to face it eventually though...won't you?"

"I guess. But..."

"Wouldn't you rather it was on your terms? He didn't come last week either. Why not be there with your chin up instead of slinking home?"

Slinking home? She had no intention of slinking anywhere. She wasn't the one who was in the wrong. Laura threw her shoulders back. "You know what? You're right. Let's go."

She ignored the muffled whispers as she and Matt wove through the throng of singles in their meeting room. She looked around for any friendly face. The only one she saw was Matt's.

"Let's sit with Kevin." He jerked his chin to where Kevin sat by himself, head in his hands.

Someone else was just as messed up by this as she was. Was this moral support or misery loving company? Did it matter?

"Hey man, we're sitting with you." Matt plopped into the chair next to his roommate.

Laura perched on the edge of the seat next to Matt and leaned around to whisper to Kevin. "You okay?"

"Sure." Kevin raised his head. "I wanted to believe her. She said there was nothing going on, that she was just trying to make sure you knew he was cheating again. But…" He gave a sardonic laugh. "More the fool me."

"I'm so sorry. I feel somewhat responsible." Laura rubbed her hands against her knees. If she hadn't dumped Ryan, would he have stopped going out with Lydia? When she'd forced the issue last time, he'd broken up with the other girl.

"There's no way any of this is your fault." Matt frowned at her before turning to Kevin. "And you need to seriously consider if the voice you heard in high school was really God or just a delusion."

"I've never been more sure of anything in my life…I guess the timing's still off." Kevin shrugged and made an effort to smile. "How are you doing? I hear you're jumping into a new salon with this guy. Guess he's actually good at cutting hair these days?"

"One of the best I've worked with. He doesn't cut your hair?"

"Not since he shaved my head bald. He's not coming near me with anything remotely sharp."

"Oh give it a rest, Kev. That was a long time ago, and a prank." Matt sighed.

"I like Mr. Ames at the barber shop on Route 29. I'm good."

Laura chuckled. "Well, when Mr. Ames finally shuffles off this mortal coil, seeing as he has to be a hundred and four by now, maybe you'll come see me. I promise not to scalp you."

"I'll think about it. Not hard, mind you, but I'll keep it in mind if I get desperate."

Matt punched Kevin's arm.

The room quieted. Laura looked toward the front, expecting to see the teacher at the podium. Her eyes grew wide. Ryan was there instead, his arm around Lydia. She started to stand but Matt's hand on her leg pushed her back into her seat.

Ryan took Lydia's other hand and spun her into his arms before dipping her backwards with a flourish. He swung her back up and spun her to his side then pressed a quick kiss to her temple to the scattered and somewhat hesitant applause of the class. Laura ignored the sidelong looks and stiffened her spine, keeping her eyes straight ahead. Her lack of coordination when it came to dancing had been a point of contention between her and Ryan since their first date. Lydia had even tried to give Laura some lessons. Clearly she hadn't made enough progress for either of them. There was more to life than being able to dance.

Matt's fingers closed around hers. She gripped them, relief filling her. At least she had some support—someone who understood that there was another side to this. Laura turned and met Matt's eyes, giving his fingers a grateful squeeze. He didn't pull away like she'd expected. She left her hand in his, caring more about the comfort it brought her than any speculation it might cause.

"Laura, honey, how long are you going to let this nonsense go on?"

Laura turned, her hand on the banister, and stared slack-jawed at her mother. "Which nonsense is that?"

"This disagreement with Ryan. Honey, you've made your point and the boy is sorry. It's time to move past it and get things underway for your wedding. You're cutting it close with some of the ordering already."

"Dad!" Laura waited until her father ambled into the hallway and looked at her with confusion. "I'm going to say this one more time, to both of you, and then I don't want it coming up again. Ryan and I are over. Done. Finished. I'm not forgiving him and moving on as if nothing has happened. He's cheated on me twice now that I know about. And frankly, I suspect there have been others that I was just too blind to see. Today in small group, he kissed Lydia in front of God and everyone. Even if you two don't think I deserve better, I do."

"But honey, didn't you listen to the sermon today?" Her mother glanced at her father for support. "It seemed so well timed, like a sign from heaven."

Laura snapped her mouth closed on a retort when her father's mouth opened.

"If you'd listened more closely to the sermon, Diane, I'm not sure we'd be standing here. Yes, the topic was forgiveness—and yes, Laura, you need to forgive Ryan, for your own sake if nothing else—but at no time did Pastor Brown say anything about continuing in abusive relationships in the name of forgiveness. All he said was that we need to forgive so that bitterness doesn't take over and ruin our lives. He was very clear to point out that forgiveness doesn't always mean restoring the relationship. And in this instance, I have to side with Laura. I never liked that boy. I stood by because I thought she loved him and because you pushed me to keep my peace the first time he nearly broke her heart. But I'm grateful he'll not be my son-in-law. Now, Laura's made herself clear. She's an intelligent, capable young woman, and I suggest you honor her wishes." He gave his wife a stern look before heading back toward the den where faint sounds from the television could be heard floating down the hall.

Laura sat on the bottom step of the stairs and looked at her mother. "I know you mean well. But even if I don't end up married, I'm going to be okay. I have to believe I'm going to be better off not married to anyone than I would be married to Ryan. How do you marry someone, stay with someone, you can't trust?"

Diane's face fell. "You'd learn to trust him again."

"Would I, Mom? Really?" She didn't see how. Not when this had happened before. Getting past his first betrayal had taken everything she had in her. She'd really only started to believe they had a future together when he proposed. And maybe that's why he'd done it. She didn't know, and didn't care enough to find out.

"I just want you to be happy. You invested so much time in him...it seems a shame to throw it away."

"I'm not the one who threw it away. He did. Now I'm going to invest my time and effort in something that matters. You remember I mentioned the salon Matthew Stephenson was thinking about starting? Well I'm going to be his business partner. You and dad always wanted me to do what I was good at, and this is it."

"Are you..." Diane trailed off at Laura's look. "Okay. I know you're not a child anymore."

"You're right, I'm not. Which leads me to the next thing I've been thinking a lot about lately. When I was getting married in June, it made sense to live at home until then. Now that I'm not, well, I'm going to find my own place. Probably with some roommates because I still want to be able to invest as much time and money into the salon as I can, but I think it's time I left home."

Chapter 9

Between meetings with lawyers for setting up the business entity for the salon, lawyer meetings for dealing with Brenda, as well as negotiations with the bank and the property owner, Laura's days were full and the month of February slipped by. Now, brave green shoots were poking their heads above ground and the grass everywhere was transitioning from the mud-brown of dormancy to the pale lime of spring. Tight buds bumped out along the trees that lined the parking lot of the strip mall. She couldn't remember if they were cherry or ornamental pear, but Laura was looking forward to seeing them in full bloom. Maybe another month, if the temperatures stayed warm.

She parked in front of the salon space and grinned. She and Matt had signed the closing paperwork last night. They'd managed to get the price down by about twenty percent and though it was still an amount that made her struggle to breathe if she thought about it too long, she knew they'd gotten a steal. The empty salon had been the only space not sold, and the owner was beginning to panic. Apparently it was difficult to sell a single strip location to a property management company, particularly when all the surrounding stores were independently owned. Bad for him, but good for them.

She slid from the car and jingled the ring of keys. She was not only a partner in a salon and spa, but a co-owner of their very own location. She turned when an engine revved then cut off. Matt hopped out of his car.

"Can you believe it's ours?" His long stride swallowed the distance between them.

"Not yet. Maybe once we're inside and we see how much work there is to do."

"Get that door open, girl, and let's see what we've got."

With a laugh, Laura opened the two locks and pulled on the door. As it swung open, Matt lifted her into his arms and spun her across the threshold. He dropped her to her feet and grinned.

"Your salon, madam."

"Goofball." Laura swatted his arm and ducked her head to hide the flush that flamed across her cheeks. Even his most casual touch left her electrified for the rest of the day. "Oh. My clipboard. I left it in the car."

She ran back out to the car and took a moment, pretending to dig through the papers on her passenger seat, despite the fact that what she needed was right on top. When she was more settled, she collected the clipboard and a paint color fan and returned to stand next to Matt.

Laura clicked her pen. "All right. Now we can start."

They spent the next four hours walking through the space to determine what each section should be, what changes they needed to have made, and prioritizing those changes. As the clock rolled around to noon, Laura had three pages of notes.

"What time is the architect getting here?" She pressed her hand into her growling stomach.

"Not until one. It being Saturday, he had some errands this morning. Want to grab a bite and relax for a few minutes before then? I think we probably have everything we need for the meeting."

"Absolutely." She sank to the floor and leaned against the wall, stretching her legs in front of her. "I'll wait here. Just make sure whatever you get me comes with a huge cup of tea."

Matt chuckled. "No complaining about what you get if you don't come along."

Laura drew an X over her heart and smiled, shooing him out the door. "Go. I'm hungry."

She watched him shaking his head as he left, angling across the parking lot. That probably meant sandwiches from the deli they'd visited when they first looked at the building. Since the sandwich she'd had then was tasty, whatever he brought back would likely be fine this time as well. This gave her a few minutes to start the hunt for a new place to live. With all the startup madness for the salon, she'd had only a few minutes here and there to even think about it, let alone follow through.

Laura leaned over to where she'd dropped her purse and fished out her cell phone. She had one reasonable lead. There was a group of girls at the church who were looking for a fourth roommate for a townhouse. She wasn't terribly excited about having three roommates, but it did significantly lower the rent. And with the work the salon was going to need, it wasn't as if she'd be home all that often. The major problem was that she didn't know any of the girls already. She'd thought she was at least familiar with all the single women at the church—being friends with the pastor's daughter tended to ensure that. So what did it mean that she had no clue who they were? Mulling it over wasn't going to answer the question. Nor would it get her a place to live. She tapped out a quick email inquiry and poked send just as Matt returned with a shopping bag bearing the logo of the deli across the parking lot.

"Got you a Reuben and large sweet tea, as ordered. Plus chips and a cookie. Cause I figure we're working hard enough that you deserve them." Matt dropped to the floor next to her and glanced at her phone. "Who ya' emailing?"

Laura tucked the phone into her pocket and held out her hand for her sandwich. "Some girls at church looking for another roommate. In January I told my parents I was moving out, but I just haven't had time this last month to do any serious looking. I happened to see their posting on the bulletin board by the church office last week. So..." she shrugged, "I guess we'll see."

"Hmm. I'd forgotten about that board. I should put a listing up there myself."

"Do you and Kevin even have room for a third person?" She sipped her tea and closed her eyes, delighted, as the tangy sweetness hit her tongue.

Matt groaned. "Remember how I said he'd been thinking of buying a house but then with Lydia and Ryan..." he flashed an apologetic grimace, "I thought he'd given up on the idea. But apparently not. He found a place he really likes, says he can see their kids running around in the yard and so forth...so come September I either need a new place myself or a new roommate."

"Whose kids? You lost me."

"His and Lydia's. You remember that youth retreat the summer before Senior year? Right after the car accident?"

Laura nodded. Though she hadn't remembered the car accident until he mentioned it. Matt had spent the bulk of the fall of their Senior year on crutches, and on the bench at football games, to the sorrow of the entire school.

"Kevin says he heard God speak to him the last night, at the bonfire, and that God told him he and Lydia would end up married."

"Huh. Well, good luck to him. He's not angling for power and money with his career choices, so I can't see how he'll catch her eye." She winced. "That was uncharitable. In the past I would have said she's not a bad person...she's just shallow. Which actually makes her and Ryan a perfect couple."

Matt laughed. "I can't disagree, though I am sorry they hurt you like they did." He bumped her shoulder with his. "I'll admit that I'm bummed Kevin didn't ask if I wanted to move with him. I mean come on, an actual house? But apparently he's also ready to rattle around in his own space."

Laura shook her head. "You and I are entirely too people-oriented to be happy in a big house with no one else around. But you've got to think about Kevin. He really is the ideal computer programmer. He enjoys being on his own, having his own space. He'll thrive on it and surface for friend time when he needs it."

"I hadn't thought of that...wonder if I've been crowding him too much. I try to respect when he's in his room, but lately I've been dragging him downstairs to talk salon business. Maybe I owe him an apology."

Laura balled up her sandwich wrapper and wiped her mouth. "Maybe so. But at least you've got some time to find someone else or another place. Which I guess I do, too. Mom and Dad aren't asking me to leave. I just figure if I'm not getting married, it's probably time to leave the nest, you know? I'm a business owner," she grinned, "I probably shouldn't still live at home."

Matt pursed his lips and appeared to give the matter considerable thought before he nodded. He looked like he was about to speak when the door rattled, followed by a knock on the glass when it didn't open.

Laura checked her watch. "He's a little early, if that's the architect?"

"That's him. And early is pretty typical for him." He pushed himself to his feet and crossed to open the door. "David, good to see you."

"Hey man." David slid off his sunglasses and looked around the space with a considering expression on his face. "I can see why you wanted it. This has good light, pretty decent bones. Hope you're not thinking of doing too much."

"Not really, no. But before we get to that, let me introduce my business partner, Laura Willis. Laura, this is David Harrington."

Laura smiled and extended her hand. "Pleasure to meet you." She ignored the speculative look David shot Matt. Any stray feelings she might be dealing with were certainly not reciprocated. Besides, they were business partners. There was no way she was going to gum up the works by trying to make it be anything else.

Matt had already begun describing the changes they were hoping for, gesturing broadly and offering the rough sketches they'd worked up. Laura pulled her attention back to the conversation. Now was the time to focus, not daydream about impossibilities.

Laura collected her decaf mocha from the end of the coffee bar and looked around. All the comfortable seats were taken, but the tables were open. She was a few minutes early for her meeting with two of the three girls in the town house. As much as she wanted to move out, and do it in an affordable way that made sense, she wasn't sure about rooming with three other women. She sat at the table by the window and watched the cars in the parking lot. Would she recognize them when she saw them? Despite the fact that it was a big church, she'd gone there practically her whole life and it bothered her that she didn't have even a vague recollection of a face to go with the names. Stifling a yawn, she sipped her coffee. Maybe she should've gotten regular instead of decaf.

The afternoon had gone well and David had seemed positive he could come up with drawings quickly. She still wasn't quite clear on how Matt knew him, but it didn't matter all that much. She trusted her business partner. Besides, David was doing the drawings in his spare time, not through his firm, so they were saving quite a bit on that end of things. He'd said he might have some construction contacts to pass along as well. If it all came through like it was starting to sound like it might...the end of May was a real possibility for a grand opening. That was still three months doing hair at people's homes or in a noisy, and potentially messy, under-construction salon. But she'd make it work. So far, her clients had understood.

She looked up when the bell on the door chimed and two young women, clearly sisters, entered. Even though there was a family resemblance, they were a study in opposites. One was dark-haired and hovered a scant few inches above the five foot mark, reminding Laura of one of Tinkerbelle's pixie friends. The other was taller, close to six feet if the strip on the door was accurate, not heavy, but solid, with red hair that was a color no chemist could ever concoct correctly. Laura sighed wistfully. She'd give anything to find a formula for red that looked natural. *That* would certainly set their salon apart.

The two girls were whispering and looking around. Their eyes kept darting to her table. Laura chewed on her lip. They couldn't possibly be who she was meeting. They barely looked old enough to drive. They approached her table, the taller one decisively, the shorter seeming a bit more reserved, though she spoke first.

"Are you Laura?"

What had she gotten into? She didn't want to be a house mother. She forced her lips into a smile and nodded. "Yes. Hi. You're June?"

The dark haired girl shot the red-head a triumphant grin. "I am. This is my sister, July."

"Hi." July turned to June as she pulled out the chair opposite Laura, "Your turn for drinks."

Rolling her eyes, June headed toward the counter to order.

"So you're sisters? How far apart are you?"

"About seven minutes. Though we did end up with different birthdays at least."

Laura's eyes widened. "You're twins?"

July laughed. "Yeah, it throws everyone. We just remind them of the movie with Danny DiVito. It happens."

Laura nodded. "I'm just going to throw this out so I can stop wondering. How old are you?"

"We'll be twenty this summer." June set a steaming cup in front of her sister then sat next to Laura.

She didn't have any idea what to say. She wasn't that much older, but she still couldn't place them. Of course, if they went to the college class instead of the single's group, that would explain some of it. But why hadn't she seen them in the halls?

They must have sensed some of her internal conflict because July spoke up.

"We were homeschooled, so we finished high school a little early. Since we've always been a bit..."

"Precocious. That's the word I prefer," June interrupted.

"Okay, we'll go with that. Precocious, we went on to college right away. Which means we graduated in December..."

"Also a little early." June nodded to emphasize her point.

July continued, "Since our fiancés won't graduate 'til May, we thought we'd come out here, plan the wedding, start our jobs...that kind of thing."

"But since we don't want to leave Ginger in too much of a lurch..."

"Ginger's the other roommate."

"Right. We wanted to make sure we had four roommates to provide a sort of cushion."

"For when we leave in July."

"After we get married."

Laura's head was beginning to hurt. Listening to them was like watching a tennis match. Or ping pong. "Do either of you ever get to say a complete sentence?"

The girls laughed.

"Sometimes." June sipped her coffee. "It's annoying, I'm sorry."

"Not annoying. Just…odd." Laura flicked the edge of her cup's heat shield with her thumb. "So you're not originally from around here?"

"No. We grew up near Chicago, stayed semi-local for college. But the boys have job offers out this way when they graduate so…" July shrugged.

"That might explain why I couldn't place you then. I've been wracking my brain trying. But if you haven't been at the church long, that makes more sense."

"So. Let's talk about the house and see if it's going to be a good fit."

Chapter 10

"So what do you think?" Matt mopped his face with the front of his shirt.

David tucked the basketball under his arm. "About Laura or the salon?"

Matt shook his head. "The salon. There's nothing to think about Laura." There couldn't be. They were friends. Business partners. And she'd gotten un-engaged just six weeks ago.

David bounced the ball to Matt. "You're not seeing what I was seeing. Or maybe you are and you're just not interested?"

Matt said nothing as he dribbled the ball in place. Was there something to see? He certainly hadn't picked up on anything from her. And this was ridiculous. She was still mourning Ryan, no matter how little he deserved it. They'd been together since high school. He faked a move to the left then jogged down the half-court for a perfect layup.

David caught the rebound. "Fine. I'm not going to push other than to say she's cute and seems to have a good head for business. You could do much worse. As to the salon," he turned his shoulder to avoid Matt's attempt to steal the ball and tossed it toward the basket, frowning as it bounced off the net-less rim, "the changes you want are straightforward and will make a good space great. I should be able to get drawings put together in a week. Maybe less. I don't have a ton going on in the evenings and Renee's ok with me doing work as long as we're hanging out in the same room."

"You're really living the dream, aren't you?"

David laughed. "I am. When are you going to find the right girl and settle down?"

Matt dribbled the ball and shrugged. "I keep waiting for God to make it clear who that right girl is. So far there haven't been any lightning bolts." He caught the ball and jumped up, shooting it through the hoop from just outside the three-point line. "Swish."

"No net, but nice shot. Why are we doing this again? I was no good at basketball when I was younger." David caught the ball Matt threw across the court. "Can we get food now? Please?"

Matt chuckled. "Kevin said he might throw some burgers on the grill if you want simple."

"That'll work. Renee's not going to be home 'til after ten. This beats an empty house hands down."

"Though you could be starting on some salon drawings." Matt dropped the ball into his gym bag and scooped the whole thing from the edge of the court.

"Of course, but those are percolating. And my client promised he wasn't going to be pushy since I'm doing him a favor."

"All right, all right. I'll call Kevin and let him know we're on the way. You remember where it is?"

"Yeah. See you in five."

"Dinner was great, thanks Kev." Matt tipped back in his chair and propped his feet on the rail of the deck.

"Agreed." David pushed his paper plate to the middle of the table and leaned back in his seat.

"Thanks. I figure I'll have a 'come see the new house' cookout in a few months. Maybe try my hand at a few more adventurous grilling items. I'll make sure Matt gets you an invite."

"A few months?" Matt shook his head. He wasn't ready to move out of this place, and finding another roommate that quickly seemed like a long shot. "I thought you were going to stay 'til the lease ran out?"

Kevin sighed. "Sorry, man. The realtor said that neighborhood is heating up and if I want the house, I need to go ahead and put in my offer. So I did. They accepted it right away. We close in a month…but I'll pay my part of the rent until you can find another roommate."

"You don't have to do that. I'll figure out how to make it work."

"Living with this guy getting to be too much?" David grinned at Matt.

Kevin laughed. "No. As far as non-wife roommates go, Matt's pretty much the best."

"Gee, thanks."

"You know what I mean. But this house…it's perfect, and I know Lydia will love it, and the schools are great for kids."

David's eyebrows shot up. "I didn't realize you were that serious with anyone. Way to keep me informed, Matt."

Matt resisted the urge to laugh. "He's serious. She's not. But while the majority of us mortals have to stick with traditional means of finding our wives, Kevin got a direct word from God. Wasn't there lightning involved, too?" He regretted his tone as soon as the words came out. He didn't envy Kevin, not really. Lydia wasn't an easy person to love, and she sure wasn't making Kevin's life any easier by refusing to even consider dating him. But it was frustrating to have his life turned upside down on the remote possibility that "someday" she and Kevin would marry.

Kevin's lips thinned. "You know the story, why don't you tell it. I have some work I should get to." He stomped into the house.

"What was that?" David watched Kevin leave and looked at Matt.

"Me being a jerk. It's a sore spot with him, especially right now since Lydia's dating Laura's ex-fiancé, and she's the reason for the ex being there. And Kevin thought he was finally making progress with Lydia...but now she's relegated him firmly in best-friend territory. And I kicked where I knew it'd hurt because I'm mad."

"About?"

"Having to move, or find a new roommate who can afford an unequal split on the rent here, within a month. All because Kevin has this whim to buy a house for a woman who doesn't give him the time of day except when she needs something." David was watching him. "What? I said I was a jerk."

"I imagine it's worse because of the stress of starting your own salon. Opening a business is a difficult proposition...having the rest of your life in flux isn't going to help. Maybe mention that when you apologize." David's teeth gleamed white in the twilight as he grinned and pushed to his feet. "Speaking of apologizing, I'm going to run. I have a few chores around the house I need to have taken care of before Renee gets back. Thanks for dinner."

"Sure." Matt's feet dropped to the deck. "Let me know when you've got drawings for us."

"Will do. I can find my way out, you hang here. Get your head straight."

Matt watched David make his way through the kitchen. When he'd disappeared, Matt put his feet back up on the rail of the deck and stared up at the few stars bright enough to poke through the gleam of D.C.'s lights on the horizon. David was right, Kevin hadn't deserved that. Not that he deserved to lose his home in the middle of all that he had going on right now, either. But that wasn't Kevin's fault. He sighed and stood. It was always better to eat humble pie while it was still warm.

Matt took a spare pin from the top corner of the corkboard and poked it through the sheet advertising the space he needed to fill. After sorting things out with Kevin the night before, Matt had decided to leave open the possibility of adding a third roommate. The basement room wasn't technically a bedroom, but it did have a bathroom and sliding doors for egress, so there was no reason not to see if someone was interested. The landlord had originally billed the place as a three bedroom because of the basement setup. Plus, with three people sharing costs the rent could get split equally and Matt could take over the master suite without feeling bad about it. Not having to go down the hall to the bathroom would be nice.

"Matthew, how are you?" Mrs. Willis rested her hand on his arm. "I hear you and my daughter are going into business together."

Matt fought to keep his expression impassive despite the disapproval evident in her tone. "Yes, ma'am. Laura's such a talented stylist and has a great head for business. I couldn't do better and I'm grateful she's willing to jump in with both feet like this."

Diane's perfectly shaped eyebrows shot up under her bangs. "Well, we'll both hope she sticks with it. She seems to be turning everything upside down lately." Her eyes flicked to the cork board. "Did you and your roommate have a falling out, dear?"

Matt winced. He could hear the unspoken quotation marks around the word roommate as she said it. "Kevin's buying a house. He's getting more serious about his girlfriend and thinks things are leading to marriage. So with the market what it is, it made sense."

"Oh. Well, I hope you find someone new. All these break ups." She shook her head.

"Mrs. Willis…I'm not gay, and I'm fairly certain you know that. I did choose to style hair for a living, so I understand that it's not a typical career for a straight man…but there are a number of us out there."

"Oh of course, Matthew. Of course." She offered a knowing smirk and another perfunctory pat to his arm before waving and calling out to someone down the hall.

Matt watched her weave through the streams of people as Sunday school classes let out and the halls filled. Who else thought that about him? It'd sure be nice if he could afford to live on his own. Then at least one avenue for speculation would be closed. He pushed away the niggling worry that finding a roommate would be harder if more people felt that way and scanned the crowds for Laura. After her mother's comment, he really didn't want to sit next to Kevin by himself.

Chapter 11

"Hey, where were you this morning?"

Laura shifted so she could hold the phone with her shoulder and closed her eyes, letting the sun warm her through the glass of her parent's sunroom. "Couldn't do it. Honestly, I started feeling ill just thinking about seeing Ryan and Lydia. So I stayed home, listened to the sermon online, and have been sitting in a sunbeam day dreaming about the salon. Did David say when we could expect drawings? I'm anxious to start getting estimates and seeing progress."

"Sometime this week. You did fine with Ryan and Lydia last week, why the issue now?"

She didn't really want to get into it. She knew it was, to a large degree, because she was starting to have feelings for Matt and she wasn't sure exactly what to do with them. She'd been with Ryan for so long it didn't seem like she should be able to get completely over him as quickly as she had. And if she jumped into a relationship with Matt, assuming of course that he was even remotely interested, would people think she'd been cheating too? She didn't want that...though on the flip side, she wasn't sure how much she cared. It might serve Ryan right to have a niggle of doubt about their relationship.

"That's a lot of thinking...anything you want to share?"

Laura chuckled. "Sorry. Not really...I can't put my finger on it, exactly. I guess maybe it's all the change right now. And you throw in the fact that the first lead on moving out didn't pan out...I feel a little like a loser. I mean really. I'm twenty-three, recently un-engaged, un-employed, and I still live with my parents. Not really where I thought I'd be at this point."

"Please. You've gotten rid of a serial-cheater who didn't deserve you, hit the wrong end of a woman whose business is failing so she took it out on you, and are in the process of becoming a successful entrepreneur. As for moving out, it's not all it's cracked up to be, trust me."

"Mom mentioned she saw you putting up a flyer at church. Kevin's really buying a house?" Laura looked out the window and watched a cardinal dash across the yard. The birds were coming out, slowly but surely. She'd have to remind Dad to pick up some seed and get the feeders put back up.

"She mention how sad she is that Kevin and I broke up?"

The sarcasm dripping off his words made her laugh. "Tell me she didn't."

"Oh, she did."

"I'm so sorry." She tried to bite back the laughter but couldn't. A snicker erupted, followed by near-hysterical guffaws that left her eyes tearing and sides aching.

"Done?"

"Sorry." Laura swallowed a final chuckle and made her voice contrite. "I'll talk to her. Again."

"Oh don't bother. People are going to believe what they want to. If it helps any, she seemed to think Kevin was using a girlfriend as an excuse to look legitimate. Honestly, part of me wonders why, if she really thinks that about me, she hasn't called the pastor."

"Let's hope that idea doesn't occur to her, okay? You really don't need the extra ridiculousness right now. Anyway, new subject. What's your week at Brenda's look like?"

Matt groaned. "Let's not go there, either. It's a nice day...you want to maybe go for a walk?"

Laura glanced down at the ratty jeans and faded striped shirt she'd pulled on. At least she'd taken a shower. She could change quickly enough. And it was a walk. Not a date. Just friends exploring the great outdoors together. Or at least exploring the oh-so-exciting sidewalks of a suburban neighborhood. "Why not."

"Cool. I'll pick you up in, say, twenty minutes? Wear sneakers."

Laura's feet ached. Between a full day of clients, none of whom seemed to have taken lots of standing into consideration when choosing their kitchen floors, and yesterday's hike at Great Falls Park with Matt, her toes were feeling abused. Her lips curved involuntarily. She'd always enjoyed watching the Potomac River throw itself over the rocks at Great Falls, but she usually limited her river watching to the falls right near the visitor center. Matt had convinced her that some of the views involving a bit of a hike were better. He'd been right about the views, but one of them didn't understand what "a bit of a hike" meant.

They'd talked about everything, and nothing. It was the easiest conversation she'd had in a long time. Nothing stilted, nothing forced. No long, awkward silences. Even when there'd been silence, it had been warm, companionable. Why had she never noticed she didn't have that with Ryan? Had she even known it was possible to have such an easy time with a man? The hike had alleviated any remaining fear about their business partnership. But it had also stirred something she wasn't ready to deal with. Could they date and be business partners? What happened if things didn't work out—business or relationship, either one?

She rested her forehead on the steering wheel. She should go home. She didn't want to. Before she could stop herself, she grabbed her phone and hit the first speed dial.

"Hello?"

Matt's voice made everything in her relax. She was going to have to figure out what, if anything, there was to do about that before much longer. "Hey, it's Laura. When do you finish up today?"

"I'm sweeping up as we speak. My last client just left and I'm not taking walk-ins today. That's a new fun policy—she has a rotation schedule for who gets walk-ins, regardless of busyness."

"That makes no sense."

"Tell me about it." There was some banging in the background and Laura imagined him tucking the broom into the supply closet and kicking it shut. "Okay, I'm out of Brenda's House of Horrible. I'm rapidly appreciating the fact that we've moved our timetable up. The sooner I'm done there, the better."

Laura chuckled.

"What's up? We didn't have a meeting planned, did we?"

"No. I was actually wondering if you might want to grab a bite to eat? I'll be honest…I don't want to go home." She winced. She hadn't meant it to sound like he was a last ditch effort to avoid something unpleasant. But backpedaling was only going to make it worse. She knew that from experience.

"I'm going to choose to take that in a more positive light than it sounded. Hmm." There was a long pause. Laura heard traffic noise before the thump of his car door cut it off. "Why don't you come over? I'm pretty sure Kevin's going to be home, but it's my turn to cook and I can easily add a third plate to the table. I'm trying to limit eating out as much as I can with all the business expenses."

"Smart. That's smart. You don't think Kevin'll mind?"

"Don't really care if he does, honestly. You're my friend and I'm extending the invite."

"Okay. See you in a bit. Can I stop and get something?"

"I don't have anything planned for dessert."

"Say no more. See you soon." She hit end and tossed her phone on her passenger seat. A friendly dinner, that's all this was. He'd said that. She knew it. She wasn't sure why it left a lump in her throat that just wouldn't be swallowed. There was a grocery store on the way that had excellent tiramisu. Coffee-laden cookies with custard sounded like just the thing to soothe the ache of being firmly relegated to the friend zone.

Matt slid a plate of garlic bread across the table to Laura. "So, it turns out Kevin's got a work thing. On the plus side, it means more lasagna for me tomorrow."

Laura laughed. He'd taken the time to light a candle in the middle of the table. It was a pine scented one, but it was still a nice touch. Would he have done that even if Kevin had been here? Was this just friends eating dinner? The mixed signals were driving her crazy. Unless there weren't mixed signals and she was just seeing them because she wanted to. "This is good. Did you make it?"

He grinned. "I did. I've been trying a few new things here and there—figured it's never a bad idea to know your way around the kitchen. There are so many recipe sites online it's crazy."

"I knew that. I'll admit to being surprised that *you* know that."

"Yeah, well." Matt shrugged. "Anyway, this was an experiment in making things ahead so all you have to do is put it in the oven. I prepped a few things on Saturday...what?"

"Nothing. I said nothing." Laura fought a grin. He was so cute. Why had she never noticed how attractive he was? Ryan. She'd been blinded by Ryan.

First that he'd pay her any attention in high school and then they were an item. She didn't think she should be looking around when she was committed to someone else. She forked a bite, eyebrows lifting as the mozzarella strings stretched from her plate to her mouth. "Mmm. Next time you make this, let me know. I'm coming over."

"Deal."

"What's new at Brenda's? I miss hearing about everyone. I didn't think I would—sometimes the drama gets to be so much, you know? But now...I feel out of the loop."

"I understand. We'll have our own gossip loop soon enough." He frowned. "Janelle quit today. She just renewed her lease, too, and Brenda was screeching at her all the way out the door, threatening legal action."

Laura's brow lifted. "I'll give her a call tomorrow with the name of my attorney. He got Brenda to toe the line of the contract eviction clause plus some. He ought to be able to help if Brenda gets on a tear about the early termination clauses. Did Janelle say where she's headed?"

"I didn't hear it if she did. I'm not sure she has anything lined up, actually. Just got to be too much. I think all of us, well all of us who aren't Brenda's lap dogs, are rapidly getting fed up. I've got Janelle's contact info somewhere. She was one I had an eye on anyway, for when we start looking to hire."

"Glad we're on the same page. Janelle's good at her job. She could maybe use a little training with color, but as far as styling goes, she's great."

Matt filled her in on the other salon gossip and Brenda's continued ridiculousness. She didn't know why she was surprised by some of what he said. Something was clearly going on with Brenda, it was just too bad that she'd chosen this method of dealing with it. If she'd come to her stylists and explained...well, the salon had always treated one another like family. Laura had no doubt they would have rallied behind Brenda, given the chance.

After dinner, they took their dessert out onto the deck. It was a little cooler than she would've liked, but the fresh smell of the approaching spring made it worth some discomfort.

"Thanks for dinner. I wasn't looking forward to dealing with my mom. Driving from one client's house to another is annoying, especially since I feel like I need to do considerable cleanup before I leave. So I'm not just cutting and sweeping up hair, I'm mopping kitchen floors all day. And now that I put it out there that I want to move out, it's like she's got one foot planted in the small of my back, pushing me out the door."

"Any prospects?"

She shook her head. "Nope. The only lead I really had was the one on Saturday. And that just didn't feel right. The sisters I met seemed nice enough, and the third roommate they mentioned is probably fine as well. But the sisters are both getting married in June…and maybe it's part jealousy that their lives are working out the way I thought mine was going to, but I don't want to be around that. If nothing else, I can't imagine it'd be a particularly restful place to go after a day spent starting up a new salon." She sighed. "What I'd love is my own place. Just me. Maybe a cat. But I can't justify the expense right now."

"I get that. Other than that cat, at least. I don't know that I'll ever get voluntarily living with something that thinks it owns you. Now a dog, I could see a dog. That's love and companionship right there."

Laura laughed. "Dogs are great if you have a schedule that'll accommodate their neediness."

"There's that."

"What about you? Any nibbles on your roommate needs?"

"Not yet." The phone in the kitchen began to ring as he started to speak. "Hold that thought."

She watched him disappear then turned back to stare across the small yards to the next row of townhouses. Lights in the windows let her peek into the lives of the families there. Some were gathered at the kitchen counter, eating and laughing with one another. In others, she could just make out the blue flicker of a TV. Just the everyday family things. She wanted that for herself. But after her colossal misjudgment of Ryan, how could she trust herself to make a decision like that again?

Matt came back out holding his laptop and grinning. "Great news. That was David. Apparently he got inspired in the middle of the night and," he sat and clicked a few things on the screen, "we now have drawings."

Laura clapped her hands and scooted closer so she could see the screen. They spent several minutes going over the drawings and the estimates that he'd included along with contractor suggestions and what he thought their prices should end up being.

"I'll get on the phone tomorrow and start scheduling some meetings." She grinned and turned to Matt, nearly bumping his nose with hers. She drew in a quick breath as her heart sped up, their gazes locking. Swallowing forcibly, she scooted back. "It's really happening."

Matt nodded.

"Hey." Kevin poked his head out the patio doors. "Can I have some of that dessert? It looks amazing."

She didn't know whether to thank Kevin or be mad. The brief awkwardness was gone, but she wondered if Matt had felt the same thing she had.

"Um, sure. I was going to leave it for you two anyway." Laura pushed her chair back and stood. "Do I have those in my email too?"

Matt nodded again. Why didn't he say something?

"Okay. Well...I should probably go. Thanks for dinner, Matt. I'll touch base tomorrow." She fled. There was no other possible way to describe the speed with which she gathered her things and made it to the car. Kevin had to be wondering what was going on, but then, so was she. Had she really almost kissed him? She didn't know if she should be disappointed or relieved that she hadn't.

At the end of the next block, Laura pulled the car to the curb and dropped her head in her hands. She shouldn't be thinking this way. He clearly wasn't. At least, the deer-in-the-headlights look and utter silence certainly suggested that was the case. She'd just focus on the renovations and getting the salon put together as quickly as she could. Then they could get back on the co-worker footing they understood.

Chapter 12

"Did I interrupt something?" Kevin brought a bowl of tiramisu out onto the deck.

"No." Matt cleared his throat. The answer had to be no, right? There'd been that moment…and he was letting his imagination run too wild. "We were just looking over David's drawings for the salon. How was your work thing?"

Kevin frowned as he scooped up a bite. "Hard to say at this point. I think it went well, but we're looking at possibly partnering with an office in London and also, maybe, outsourcing some things to India. I'm not one hundred percent on board with the idea of outsourcing but it seems to be the way the world is moving right now."

"Will that impact your job?"

"Shouldn't, no…why'd she run off like that?"

Matt rubbed a hand over his face. "I…we had a moment."

Kevin quirked a brow. "A moment?"

Matt shot his friend a look. "Yeah. We were both looking at the drawings and she turned and…" He groaned. "It was all I could do not to kiss her. And I didn't get the feeling she'd be too upset if I did."

"So why didn't you?"

"Where do I start? She broke off her engagement to the only guy she's dated since high school. How 'bout there?"

"And? All I'm hearing is that she's single and unattached. And you're interested. Which, I'll admit, I find interesting. Particularly since you enjoy accusing me of carrying a torch for someone unattainable." Kevin poked Matt's shoulder. "Pot." He flipped his finger toward himself. "Kettle."

"It's not the same. I haven't…" Matt narrowed his eyes. "You're messing with me, aren't you?"

Kevin grinned. "Maybe a little. Doesn't change the fact that if you're interested in Laura I think you ought to do something about it."

Matt frowned. All the reasons that wasn't the world's best advice zipped through his mind. If he forced himself to be brutally honest, he'd admit he was worried he was misreading the situation. He valued her friendship too much to risk anything else. Plus there was the new salon to consider. What if he asked her out, made it clear that he was asking her on a date, and she said no? Could they still co-own a salon if their personal relationship changed for the worse?

"I'll think about it."

"Do that. In the mean time, Mario Kart?"

Matt pushed thoughts of Laura to the back of his mind. He wasn't going to figure out what to do tonight anyway. "Sure. I haven't creamed you in a few weeks."

The rest of the week was a combination of long days at the salon and late nights at the new space going over bids and equipment orders with Laura. Most days she brought dinner with her, and the two of them ate on a rickety card table in the back room while they settled on contractors, colors, and styles. Matt was impressed with the clear vision Laura had for the salon. He'd had vague ideas about decorating schemes, but hadn't taken them any further than that, planning, when he thought about it at all, to hire a decorator when the time came.

Looking at the poster board collage Laura had tacked to the wall, he smiled. The overall effect was a subtle trip to the islands. Soothing teals mixed with creams and tans on the walls and upholstery. Dark woods for the stations and floors complimented the colors and brought the theme together. Even the main area of the salon, which would need better lighting from a practical standpoint, had the same relaxed feel. If they could translate the ideas into reality, their salon was going to be the perfect mixture of relaxation and function. He even liked the idea of suspending mirrors from the ceiling to separate stations and provide stylist space on either side.

Matt checked his watch. He expected Laura to be here already. It wasn't like her to be late. He hoped nothing was wrong. He had the final contracts for various workers they were going to need and wanted to get them signed and faxed over tonight. He'd been assured that the offices were open on Saturday, so they'd get the faxes the next day and then, if all went well, they could get the work started on Monday or Tuesday. The way things were going at Brenda's, he'd be surprised if anyone stuck around much longer. The only thing keeping him there at this point was the salon and the fact that his lease ended in April. He could try and juggle home visits like Laura, but he'd just as soon keep the status quo for another month if he could.

He was checking his watch again when Laura rushed in, hugging a binder to her chest. Papers flapped around the edge of the notebook, looking like they were going to fly out at any moment. She dropped the notebook on the table. "Sorry I'm late. I got suckered into a second color job at Mrs. Yardly's. Her neighbor just happened to be over visiting." She rolled her eyes. "On the positive side, I probably have a new repeat client and they're both excited about the salon opening."

"All's well that ends well, right?"

"Exactly. I didn't want to say no, if only because the poor woman really needed her color done. It was tragic. And I didn't want to sneak off and call— you've heard Mrs. Yardly go on about cell phones, right?"

Matt laughed. "I have, indeed. It's no biggie. I was just starting to get a little concerned."

"Unfortunately in all the rush, I didn't have time to get home and do anything about dinner. I thought about picking something up, but…I just wanted to get here and sit down. Maybe take off my shoes." She slid into the folding chair across from Matt and eased her feet from her clogs.

"It's Friday night…why don't we go to dinner after we get our business taken care of?" Her expression was hard to read. What was she thinking? "Unless you have plans…"

"No. No plans. And I'd like that. Sorry, long day." She looked down at the stack of bids spread out on the table. "What do we have here?"

They spent several minutes weighing the pros and cons of the drywall contractor bids and finally came to the conclusion that the price difference was small enough they should just use who David recommended. Sometimes you really do get what you pay for, and Matt knew drywall was one of those things that could look terrible if it wasn't done right. Since he had no interest in trying to learn how to fix it, he convinced Laura to spend a little more for someone who was recommended by an industry professional, not just the phone book.

Matt tapped the short pile of signed bids, evening the edges. "Anything else?"

Laura flipped open her binder and slid a dog-eared and sticky-note laden catalog across to him. "This has the furnishings I think we ought to use throughout. The sticky notes explain what I'm thinking and," she shuffled through a few more pages, "this is a rough estimate for cost. No, look at it later. When you have a comfortable place to pass out for a minute or two."

Matt's laugh trailed off as his eyes found the bottom line. "Yowch. Really?"

She lifted a shoulder. "We want upscale clients. We're offering upscale services. I think we have to be willing to make an initial investment to reflect that."

"It's a reasonable argument. I'll look through this more carefully tonight."

"One more thing." Laura took a small packet of papers held together with a binder clip out of the notebook. "These are resumes I think we should consider. I know we don't need a ton of stylists out of the gate. Between you and me, we should be able to handle things initially with maybe one or two part-timers. But we will need spa staff and a receptionist. So that's what I've been focusing on. If we have one good nail tech and one to do massages, wraps, and facials then we should be set for at least the first six months.

We can reevaluate as we see how the appointments are going."

"Perfect. I'll look through these, too. Do you have your favorites noted in here?"

"Thought about it but decided I'd rather see how closely we agree." She flashed a grin.

"A test, hmm? Well. I definitely need to eat if I have a test on the horizon. Ready to go?"

"Almost. Since we're going to have work starting soon, hopefully next week, and I'll need to be here to supervise, is it all right with you if I have my clients come here? I think I can set up a reasonable enough station out of the way that everyone will be happy."

"As long as it's not getting in the way of the workers and your clients don't mind, I have no problem with it. Beats you driving all over creation. It will be noisy and dusty though. Make sure that will work. Now come on. Let's go in my car, I'll drop you back here when we're done."

Chapter 13

"Laura, is that you?"

Laura sighed and dropped her purse and overstuffed backpack at the foot of the stairs. Of course it was too much to ask for her mother not to hear her come in. She kicked off her shoes and padded down the hall to the den. Her mom and were dad cuddled together on the sofa. Her lips turned up. "Hi."

Diane patted the space at the end of the couch by her feet. "Join us for a bit? You're home earlier than usual."

Laura perched on the arm of the sofa. She didn't want to sit and watch game shows with her parents. She wanted to go up to her room, soak her feet, and go to sleep. "We didn't have much to do tonight. Just a few bids to decide between and then fax, plus I gave Matt some details on possible staff and the furnishings I think we ought to choose. He'll need to be okay with both though, so he's got the info to mull for the weekend, or whatever. It's not like we need to move on either immediately. It'll be at least a month, probably longer, before the construction's finished."

Her dad smiled and hit the mute button on the TV as it switched to commercials. "That's the most animated I've heard you in a while, sweetie. It's good to see you getting back to yourself. This business, and your business partner, are good for you."

"Thanks, Dad."

"Any new developments on finding a place?"

Laura considered her mother's expression. Was she trying to kick her out? Or was she simply curious? She didn't know how to read her mother anymore, because she had no idea. It was probably better not to delve too deeply anyway. "Nope. Haven't seen anything I've even wanted to follow up on, to be honest. You might be stuck with me a while longer. At least 'til the salon opens and I see if I'll be able to swing a place on my own."

"You know we love having you, don't you?"

"I know, Dad. I still feel like it's time to be on my own, but I appreciate you letting me take the time to find the right place."

"How's Matthew dealing with his breakup?" Diane's face was the picture of sympathy.

Laura closed her eyes. "There's no breakup for him to be dealing with, Mom. Kevin's buying a house because he's in love with Lydia, has been since high school for whatever reason, and he seems to think this is a smart move on his part. This leaves Matt, a wonderful, Godly, heterosexual hairdresser looking for a new roommate or roommates so he doesn't have to move out of his home while he's in the midst of opening a new salon with me. Honestly, in a perfect world, where it wouldn't be completely misconstrued, *I'd* be his roommate."

Both of her parents drew their breath in sharply.

"Laura! Don't even joke about moving in with a man. You were raised better than that."

Laura wanted to laugh at the shock on her mother's face. She also wanted to ask why, if Matt wasn't interested in girls, it would matter. But of course she knew he was and it was better not to try and use logic to argue with the irrational. She met her dad's eyes and saw the laugh sparkling in them. At least he understood the indefensible nature of her mom's position.

"I said in a perfect world. Sheesh."

"Did you eat? Your mother made pot roast and I know there are some left overs in the fridge. I was saving them for a late night snack, but I'll share if you're hungry."

Laura didn't try to stop the smile. "You're the best, Dad. But Matt and I went out after we finished our paperwork. He took me over to the rib place near church. He likes their onion loaf as much as I do." She patted her stomach. "I don't think I've eaten that well since the lasagna he made earlier this week."

Laura ignored her mother's appraising look and stood. She leaned over to kiss her dad's forehead and pressed her cheek to her mother's cheek. "I'm going to go soak my feet and get to bed. It's been a long week."

She thought about her dinner with Matt as she trudged up the stairs with her heavy bag. It had felt like a date. He'd driven, opened doors, held her chair, and insisted on paying. None of which he'd done before. Oh, sure, he didn't let a door slam in her face, but he'd never gone out of his way to get them before. And the restaurant was decidedly a date-quality venue. Was it possible he had feelings for her?

Thoughts of Ryan flooded her mind unbidden as she lowered her feet into steaming hot water. After his repeated unfaithfulness, how was she supposed to trust men who said they were interested in her? Not that Matt had, but what if he did? Just the thought of Ryan's betrayal had her muscles constricting, her teeth on edge. When would the anger go away? She knew it wasn't right, knew she had to forgive him. But she didn't want to. No matter how many times she listened to Pastor Brown's sermon reminding her that bitterness only hurt her and that forgiveness didn't mean she had to restore a relationship with either Ryan or Lydia...she preferred to hold her hurt close. And wasn't she entitled? Five years of her life she'd invested in him and for what?

She pulled her feet from the water and carefully dried them off before taking the time to massage thick, fragrant lotion into each one. Mindful of her slippery feet, she walked on her heels to her room and fell into bed. Barely after nine o'clock on a Friday night and she was done. As she drifted off, she sent up a half-hearted prayer for help forgiving Ryan and Lydia.

"Looking good." Laura watched as Matt walked through the salon, poking his head between the framed in walls and tugging on the boards.

"Yeah, they've been busy this week. David stopped by yesterday to check things out, he thought they might be finished by the end of the first week of April." Laura rubbed her hands together. She was ready to open and get on with the new phase of her life. Maybe once the salon was open she'd be able to find an affordable place to live and get out from under her mother, who kept making little snide comments about choosing to spend her time with Matt instead of just forgiving a real man who loved her. Her father had tried to step in, but that hadn't turned out overly well. It was nice to know she had his support at least.

"Wow. That's fast. Any way we could open in April?"

Laura's eyebrows lifted at the desperation evident in his tone. "Things not going well at Brenda's?"

He shook his head. "All the shampoo girls are gone. Granted, I typically did my own shampooing anyway, but on days like today when it's busy, it's nice to have some help getting the next client ready while you finish up the one in front. Instead, we got so backed up that Brenda started walking around yelling at everyone to hurry because people were waiting. Then, when the clients waiting up front started leaving, she yelled more. I got a call from one of my appointments letting me know she'd come back, but she left because of the yelling. I don't imagine she was alone in that decision."

"Ouch."

"Pretty much. I had two others ask me while in my chair, with Brenda hovering nearby mind you, if there was any chance I'd be moving somewhere else some time soon." He rolled his eyes. "I wanted to tell them about this place, but I figured that'd be all it took for Brenda to send me packing in the middle of a client's cut."

"We need business cards. That way you could just slip them one when they ask. Or even if they don't ask. We also need a website. And for all of those things, we need a name. I had a thought but it's kind of…cheesy I guess. So I wasn't sure I should share it."

"Anything that's not Matt and Laura's House of Hair or something along those lines is going to be all right with me. Let's hear it."

Heat stole up her neck and across her cheeks. Why had she mentioned her idea at all? "I'm warning you, it's stupid. But maybe it's a place to start brainstorming."

"Stop stalling, just spit it out."

Laura cleared her throat. "A Cut Above."

Matt pursed his lips, his head tilted to the side. Laura watched him. Was it so bad he couldn't come up with anything more to say? She'd at least expected him to smile, or chuckle, or something. She forced herself to hold back the tide of babble building in her throat.

After what felt like an hour, though a quick glance at her watch showed it had only been a minute, Matt grinned. "I like it. It's clever and fun and people will remember it. Let's do it."

"Really?" Laura laughed and threw her arms around him in an impromptu hug. "We have a business name."

Matt gave her a quick squeeze then eased back. The flush that was just starting to fade crept back up. What was she doing? He must think she was crazy. Who was she kidding, she was crazy. She had no business thinking about Matt like that, or touching him. They were friends and business partners. Why couldn't she get that through her head?

He cleared his throat. "So, website? That also needs a logo, right?"

She nodded and reined in her thoughts. "I found someone online who has some reasonable marketing packages that include logo creation, website set up and maintenance and that sort of thing. I've been looking at the other sites they've done and think they're pretty reasonable. Basic, but reasonable. And compared to the prices I'm seeing for other people who offer the same services, this is the way to go."

"All right, go with it. I trust your judgment. Anything more we can do around here tonight?"

She shook her head. "I ordered the furniture as soon as I got your okay and it's scheduled to be delivered in the next two weeks. I think we should be okay for installing it at that point unless we hit a major snag with the construction, but so far things are going exactly like the plan. You know...we could probably schedule our opening for the first week of May."

"Really?"

"I don't see why not. That's nearly six weeks away and the way things are going..." Laura shrugged. "I was toying with the idea of having a soft opening a day or two before our Grand Opening. Invite our current clients, maybe offer some sort of discount or complimentary service in addition to our full menu."

"I like that idea. And with a day or two before the real opening, we can make any tweaks that need to happen. Tell you what, let's give it another week and see if things continue to be on schedule, talk to David and that sort of thing and then, as soon as the website is ready, announce our grand opening and start taking appointments. Phone. We'll need to have phone service as soon as we let people know it's coming."

"I'm on it. They should be hooking us up next Friday. The construction guys said that would work as far as they could tell."

"You're the best. Have any plans for dinner?"

She couldn't stop the leap of her heart, couldn't convince herself she even wanted to. "Nope."

"Up for trying someplace new? I got a recommendation from a client and it sounds really yummy."

"Sounds great."

"Let's go. We can swing by and get your car when we're finished, it's not far."

Chapter 14

Matt waited as the Sunday school class emptied out of their meeting room. Laura was talking with a girl and her boyfriend who were visiting, but he wanted to see if she'd be up for lunch. They'd had dinner Friday night after going over the progress of the salon, as had become their habit, but he needed to tell her about his Saturday at Brenda's. He shook his head, remembering the scene she'd caused when he'd let her know he wouldn't be renewing his space rental. She'd sent him home then and there. He probably could find decent grounds for some sort of recompense, but he was so glad to be rid of the place, it didn't really matter. As it stood, their scheduled grand opening was just two weeks away. The soft opening was completely booked and their first week well on its way to the same state. They could probably use the time to finish their punch list.

"Sorry." Laura bumped his hip with hers. "The new girl, Marla, can talk. I don't get the impression Steve was overly impressed with our class though. He used the term 'meat market' at least three times."

Matt winced, though he had to admit the man had a point, at least on some level. "Well, there are plenty of other classes to try. I don't know that I'd stay here if I had a steady relationship with someone."

"Yeah, me either. So what's up? You said you had news?"

"I was hoping we could catch some lunch?"

Laura's face fell. "I can't. I promised my dad some daddy-daughter time today. Since it's nice, I'm guessing we'll end up on the golf course. Can I just tell you how not excited I am by that? But maybe he'll let me drive the cart."

Matt ignored the stab of disappointment and forced a chuckle. "Well, that should be fun. Long story short, so you can get on with your exciting afternoon, you'll have me full time for the next two weeks. Brenda didn't like my notice on Saturday and sent me on my way. I've called all my clients and given them the main salon number, so hopefully we can get them fitted in either our first official week open or, in a pinch, the night before our soft opening."

"Should be doable. I've got the computer all set up, and Casey will be in to learn the ropes for her job as receptionist this week, so having people calling in will be good." She rested her hand on his arm and gave it a light squeeze. "I have to run, but I'll see you tomorrow."

"Yep. Have fun." He laughed when she shot him a look and stuffed his hands in his pockets while he watched her weave through the crowded halls. He was sunk. There was no point in denying it any longer. At least not to himself. If this wasn't love, he had no idea what love was. He also had no idea what to do about it.

It'd been just about four months since she and Ryan broke things off. She seemed to be doing really well, but four months didn't seem like all that long compared to the years she and Ryan were together. How long did it take before it was okay to ask her out on a date? A real date. Something she knew was a date. And what if she ended up not being interested?

Matt didn't think that was the case, unless he was completely incapable of reading body language. She certainly gave off signals that indicated interest to him. And it was those signals, and the beginnings of an idea in his mind, that had him taking down his roommate advertisement a week ago. Kevin was moving out in two weeks, just in time for the grand opening, but when Matt had floated his idea, Kevin had agreed to paying his rent for at least another month, or at least until Matt had an answer one way or the other.

He nodded absently to acquaintances as he made his way to his car, his thoughts drifting to the leftovers in his fridge at home. Without Laura along, it didn't make sense to go out. If all else failed, there was a sandwich of some kind. He was pretty sure they had bread. He was so absorbed in those thoughts, he nearly plowed into Laura's mother.

"Matthew." Diane placed her hand on his chest to get him to stop. Her lips thinned and she wiped her hand discretely on her skirt before crossing her arms over her chest. "I've been waiting for you for nearly twenty minutes."

He drew his eyebrows together. "I don't recall having an appointment, Mrs. Willis. What can I do for you?"

"I'd like to know just exactly what you think you're doing. Everything with Laura these days is 'Matthew this' and 'Matthew that.' It's simply unacceptable. I won't allow my daughter to be some man's beard. That's what they call it, isn't it?"

"Now look here." Matt took a deep breath and fought to control his temper. "I've explained this to you. I know Laura has as well. I don't know what it's going to take for you to understand it, but the fact of the matter is that my choice of profession is just that, a profession. Your daughter and I are business partners and, beyond that, she's my best friend. You do both of us a disservice when you insist on stereotypes and unfounded prejudice."

Her jaw dropped then snapped shut with a sharp click. "Is that all you are?"

What did she mean by that? "At this time, yes."

"Then you need to make that clear to her. I know my daughter. I recognize the signs of infatuation. She hasn't dated anyone since her unfortunate breakup with Ryan. And while I've gotten over the fact that those two aren't going to mend fences, I won't see her end up broken hearted over a man who could never love her."

Infatuation? His heart raced. He wasn't misreading the signs. Hopefully her feelings went as deep as his own. He was way past infatuation. His lips curved. "I'll make my feelings and intentions crystal clear in the near future, Diane."

She gave a curt nod and stalked off.

Matt rubbed his hands together. He had a lot of preparation to do and a very short amount of time to do it.

Matt flopped into the client chair at his station and watched Laura flip the lock on the door as the last of the clients exited. "If how much my feet hurt is any indication, our soft opening was a huge success."

Laura laughed and sat in the chair next to his, bouncing slightly. "It was awesome. And I don't use that word lightly. There are a few tweaks to make in the appointment system—massages need to be scheduled for fifteen minutes longer than the actual massage to ensure there's time for the client to undress and redress and get the room cleaned and reset. I have a list of other tweaks somewhere. But it's not very long."

"I kept notes too. But we can compare them tomorrow. Let's get this place cleaned up and then I want to take you out somewhere nice to celebrate."

"Shouldn't we wait 'til Saturday for that?" Laura pushed out of her chair and crossed to the broom.

"Nope. We can do it again on Saturday, but tonight deserves a celebration."

Her laughter zapped through him, electrifying every nerve ending.

"Oh. My mom keeps asking me if you've told me something important yet, something to do with some conversation she had with you at church?"

Matt shrugged and hoped his expression conveyed confusion and not the anger that surged through his veins. That woman. He had a few choice words of his own he'd like to give her. Though it would serve no purpose.

"Yeah, that's what I thought. Honestly, some days I wonder if she hasn't completely lost her mind. I still find her sniffling over wedding magazines. And, okay, I get that it's disappointing. I'm disappointed, too. But I actually find I'm not having to forgive Ryan multiple times a day anymore. And I know that there's someone better out there for me." Her eyes flicked up and met his, pink stealing across her cheeks.

Did she have any idea how lovely she was? Inside and out. It was all he could do to make himself stick to his plan. But he'd put enough thought into it that he didn't want to ruin it now. He could wait two more days. He would.

"That's good to hear. I've wondered how you were doing but couldn't figure out how to ask. I didn't want to bring it up and rub salt in the wound, you know?"

She smiled and scooped debris into the dustpan. "I do know. And I should've said before how much I appreciate you being here for me, and just being someone I could talk to without having to worry about what I said or how it sounded. You let me be me, and I appreciate it more than you can possibly imagine."

Matt sprayed window cleaner on the last mirror and wiped it dry. The warmth in her tone belied any brush off he might have sensed in the words. Before he could panic, he brought to mind her mother's words. Diane might have been trying to warn him off, but all she did was cement in his mind that he had a pretty solid chance. And just like the salon, he was prepared to go all in. She was worth the risk.

Chapter 15

Laura brushed her hair one final time and gave herself a thorough once over in the mirror. It was the opening day of A Cut Above and she wanted to look perfect. She knew after the full schedule of clients, on top of managing the salon, she was going to get rumpled and mussed, but she wanted to start the day out right at least. If only for Matthew.

She wasn't sure when she'd started referring to him as Matthew in her mind. Probably about the same time she'd realized she was half in love with him and well on the way to finishing off the other half. She didn't know what to make of his actions toward her. They were friends, that much she knew. But as far as anything else went…some days she thought he felt the same, and other days she couldn't tell. It was frustrating.

But today wasn't the day to worry about it. Today was a day to celebrate their joint venture. A Cut

Above was going to be a huge success; she could feel it
in her bones.

On the drive to the salon, she drove through a
coffee shop for two large lattes. They'd have coffee on
for the clients, but she needed something to settle her
nerves. And Matthew was partial to the vanilla syrup. It
hadn't put her behind schedule, she was actually five
minutes ahead of when they'd agreed to meet, but the
lights were already on. She grabbed her bag and the
coffees and struggled to pull open the door while
clicking the lock button on her car's key fob.

"Matthew?" She frowned and set the coffees
down on the reception desk. The dark wood contrasted
with the Caribbean blue paint made her smile, as did
the faint smell of coconut from their hair products
lining the shelves along the front window. Dropping her
bag behind the desk, a flash of red caught her eye.

She frowned and walked to the entrance to the
main salon. A thick, red velvet ribbon lay on the floor,
winding between the stations toward the back room.
The corners of her mouth poked up. What was he up to?

Laura bent and picked up the end of the ribbon
and began to roll it as she followed its path through the
salon. As she rounded her chosen station, she saw a
hand printed sign taped to the back of her client chair. It
read: In three minutes, I'll remind you that you're my
best friend.

"Aww." She hadn't meant to say it aloud, but it
touched her. She smiled and water filled her eyes.

Blinking it back, she continued to roll the ribbon and follow it through the stations. Coming to the station Matthew had chosen, she wasn't surprised to see another sign. When she reached it, a tear slipped from her eye as she read his neat printing: In two minutes, I'm going to tell you for the first time that I love you.

He loved her. Did he have any idea how much she longed to hear that? How she longed to be able to tell him? She hadn't thought there was a chance, really, for them to have a future. Could she have been wrong?

She continued rolling the ribbon on her way to the office door. It stood slightly ajar, another note taped to its front: In one minute, I'm going to ask you to be my wife.

Her breath caught. The world stood still. Then, in a rush, everything came screaming back into real time. Hand shaking, she pushed open the door.

Matthew stood in the sparsely decorated room, a bouquet of roses in his hands, nervous smile playing at the corner of his mouth. The tears ran down her face as their eyes met and he took a step toward her.

Caught in the sense of unreality, she took the flowers and tucked them in her arm as he held her hands.

"Laura. You're my best friend. You have been since college, well, beauty school. But then even when I went to college, you kept that place. And then at Brenda's...I never would have lasted as long there without your friendship. Even before you and Ryan were through, I had feelings that went beyond friendship, though I tried to keep them at bay. When he was so stupid, I'll admit to being glad that maybe, just maybe I'd have a chance. And now, having worked with you on this salon, you're still my best friend. The only thing that's changed is that I love you. Every day it seems like I love you a little more. This salon is a fantastic start, but I want more. I want to spend my life with you. Will you marry me?" Matt slipped his hand in his pocket and pulled out a diamond solitaire as he dropped to one knee.

Laura sniffled and wiped her cheek with her elbow as she held out her left hand. "Of course I will. Oh, Matthew, I love you."

He slid the ring onto her finger, stood, and pulled her into his arms, crushing his mouth to hers.

Giggling, Laura pulled back and swiped again at the tears trailing down her cheeks. "We have to get ready to open."

Matt held out his hand. "It's going to be a terrific day."

Laura slipped her hand in his. "The first day of our lifelong joint venture."

THANK YOU!

I hope you enjoyed *"Joint Venture"*! I need to ask you a favor. Would you help others enjoy this book too?

Recommend it. Please help other readers find this book by recommending it to friends in person and on social media.

Review it. Reviews can be tough to come by these days. You, the reader, have the power to make or break a book. Loved it, hated it – I'd just enjoy your feedback. Please tell other readers what you thought about this book by reviewing on your favorite e-book retailers or social media.

My goal is to have 100 honest reviews.

Will you help me reach that goal?

Want a free book?

If you enjoyed *Joint Venture* and would like to read another book of mine, you can receive a free download of *Courage to Change*, simply by signing up for my newsletter here: http://bit.ly/2g0AGvf

Thank you so much for reading *"Joint Venture"* and for spending time with me.

In gratitude,
Elizabeth Maddrey

Author's Note

Matt and Laura kept reappearing in the stories of the first three Grant Us Grace novels (book one: *Wisdom to Know,* book two: *Courage to Change,* and book three: *Serenity to Accept*) and I realized they were pretty special and needed their own story told. Since I'm not a big planner when it comes to writing, it was an interesting experience to write about people who were pretty well established in the other novels. I had a lot of help tracking down errors and inconsistencies and think we've found them all – but anything missed is absolutely my own fault, not that of my fantastic editor, Lynellen Perry.

If you enjoyed Matt and Laura's story and would like to read more about them and their friends (Kevin, Lydia, and Allison all feature prominently), I hope you'll look up the three full-length 'Grant Us Grace' novels. They're available on all e-book platforms and in paperback. I hope you'll also take a moment to connect with me either on Facebook (www.Facebook.com/ElizabethMaddrey) or my website (www.ElizabethMaddrey.com).

About the Author

Elizabeth Maddrey began writing stories as soon as she could form the letters properly and has never looked back. Though her practical nature and love of math and organization steered her into computer science for college and graduate school, she has always had one or more stories in progress to occupy her free time. When she isn't writing, Elizabeth is a voracious consumer of books and has mastered the art of reading while undertaking just about any other activity. *Serenity to Accept* is her third published novel (book 3 in the *Grant Us Grace* series that begins with *Wisdom to Know* and *Courage to Change*.) She is also the co-author of *A is for Airstrip: A Missionary's Jungle Adventure*, a children's book based on the work of a Wycliffe missionary.

Elizabeth lives in the suburbs of Washington D.C. with her husband and their two incredibly active little boys. She invites you to interact with her at her website: http://www.ElizabethMaddrey.com or on Facebook: www.facebook.com/ElizabethMaddrey

www.ingramcontent.com/pod-product-compliance
Lightning Source LLC
Chambersburg PA
CBHW022133170626
46808CB00002B/969